By the Author of "John Halifax."

From the North British Review.

She attempts to show how the trials, perplexities, joys, sorrows, labors, and successes of life deepen or wither the character according to its inward bent.

She cares to teach, *not* how dishonesty is always plunging men into infinitely more complicated external difficulties than it would in real life, but how any continued insincerity gradually darkens and corrupts the very life-springs of the mind; *not* how all events conspire to crush an unreal being who is to be the "example" of the story, but how every event, adverse or fortunate, tends to strengthen and expand a high mind, and to break the springs of a selfish or merely weak and self-indulgent nature.

She does not limit herself to domestic conversations, and the mere shock of character on character; she includes a long range of events—the influence of worldly successes and failures—the risks of commercial enterprises—the power of social position—in short, the various elements of a wider economy than that generally admitted into a tale.

She has a true respect for her work, and never permits herself to "make books," and yet she has evidently very great facility in making them.

There are few writers who have exhibited a more marked progress, whether in freedom of touch or in depth of purpose, than the authoress of "The Ogilvies" and "John Halifax."

MY MOTHER AND I.

A Love Story.

"There I sat like a fool—no, like a poor creature suddenly stunned, who knew not what she said or did."—[See p. 178.]

MY MOTHER AND I.

A Love Story.

BY THE AUTHOR OF

"JOHN HALIFAX, GENTLEMAN," &c.

WITH ILLUSTRATIONS.

NEW YORK:
HARPER & BROTHERS, PUBLISHERS,
FRANKLIN SQUARE.
1874.

ILLUSTRATIONS.

MY MOTHER AND I.

CHAPTER I.

"Seventy years ago, my darling; seventy years ago."

So murmurs Tennyson's "Grandmother" to her "Little Annie," telling, without pain, the painful incidents of a long-past youth.

I have no little Annie, and it is not quite seventy years since I was a girl; but still I can understand how the old woman talked of her girlhood, and even enjoyed doing so, in a sort of way.

Revisiting lately, after a long lapse of time, a place

where I once spent six months—the six months which were the turning-point in my whole life—I see my own old self so vividly and with such a curious interest, nay, even pity, as if it were somebody else, that I half incline to tell the whole story: a story so simple, so natural, so likely to have happened, in one form or another, to many a girl, and withal so long ended, that it can do nobody any harm, and may do somebody some little good.

Poor Elma Picardy! Looking back at her, she seems to be—not me at all, but "a girl in a book." If I were to put her into a book, would she help other girls a little? Perhaps; for I believe many another girl has gone through a similar experience; has had her fate settled for good or ill before she was out of her teens; has gone through the same hard struggles, all alone, with nobody to advise or comfort her, and a cluster of extraneous folk standing by, looking on and discussing her, in the cold, wise—I mean worldly-wise—way in which elder people do discuss the young, as if they themselves had forgotten their own youth, or possibly had never had any. It is different with me. I was young once—young and foolish. I know it; yet am not ashamed of it; and it may help me to be a help to some other poor girl, who has no mother to speak to, or if she has one, would not speak to her if she could, or could not if she would, since, alas! all these cases do sometimes happen. For such a one I will write my story.

My name was Elma Picardy, as, indeed, it is still; and I was just seventeen, an only child, whose life would have been perfectly solitary except for her mother.

My mother and I. Never were there such friends as my mother and I; real equal friends, in addition to being mother and daughter. It was so from my cradle, my father having died a month after I was born. I never had a nurse-maid: she was too poor to give me one, even had she wished; but I think she did not wish. I was all she had, and she preferred keeping me wholly to herself. Besides, in those days mothers took care of their children rather more than they think it necessary to do now. It was not considered that even her duties to society compelled a lady to resign to a staff of inferior women that other duty—to bring up for God and man those precious little human souls and bodies with which Heaven had intrusted her. The world still held the old-fashioned opinion that to be a mother, in the largest sense, was at once the highest honor and the chiefest usefulness to which any woman could aspire.

So my mother, both by choice and necessity, was my only nurse, my sole playfellow. From morning till night and from night till morning we were never apart. It was, of course, an exceptional condition of things; but so it was, and I have never ceased to be thankful for the fact, and for its result, that through all my babyhood and childhood I learned absolutely nothing but what I learned from her. Afterward other people taught me; for though a well-read, she was not exactly an accomplished woman; but that was mere outside learning. My true education, the leading and guiding of soul and heart, was never in any hands but my mother's. In the course of years she ceased to be my governess, but she never ceased all her days to be, as the Bible says, "my companion, my guide, my most familiar friend."

Yes, familiar, though she was thirty when I was born. But this gulf of time did not seem to affect us. Either she slipped gently down to my level, or I stepped up to hers; I knew not how it was done, but done it was, the gulf being bridged over without any conscious effort on her side or mine. And the trust between us was equal to the sympathy. I hear girls nowadays say, "Oh, don't tell mamma; she wouldn't understand." Why, my mother understood every thing, and I always told her every thing! As soon as I could speak it was, "Look, mammy, look!" at every new felicity; and as for sorrow, from the day when I broke my doll till I broke—something else: only I did not quite break it—my first cry was, "Mother—I want my mother!" Day and night my only shelter was in her bosom. I remember, and can feel still, though I am an old woman, the infinite healing of her kiss for all anguish, great and small.

My mother was quite alone in the world, being, as I

said, widowed directly after my birth. My father was an Indian officer. From his miniature, he must have been much handsomer, and I knew he was a year or two younger, than herself. The exact circumstances of their marriage I never learned. It came probably from what I have heard called "the force of propinquity," for they must have been very unlike in every way. But they were thrown together, he having lodged at the house of her parents—he had quarreled with his own—during a long and dangerous illness. "He could not do without me—so he married me," she once said, with a rather sad smile; and this was the only explanation she ever gave, even to me, her daughter, of her courtship and marriage.

In a year death ended the union, and she was alone again—more alone than before: for her parents had died also, and died bankrupt. The few luxuries she had ever enjoyed passed away; she had nothing to live upon but the two small pensions, hers and mine, as a soldier's widow and orphan; and she had not a creature in the world belonging to her except me.

This was all I knew of her and myself during my childhood and early girlhood. She never talked to me about the past; and the present was all-sufficient, of course, to a child. Consequently she learned to make it sufficient to herself. And this, I have since thought, constituted the great blessing I unconsciously was to her. In all her cares and afflictions she "set me in the midst," as Christ once set a little child; and in my innocent ignorance, my implicit trust, my glorious forgetfulness of yesterday and indifference to to-morrow, I became to her truly "of the kingdom of heaven." As she told me long afterward, I comforted her more than she could have been comforted by any other living soul.

So we were perfectly happy together, my mother and I. We lived in a world of our own—a wonderful world, full of love, content, and enjoyment. That we were poor did not affect us in the least—poverty never does much affect a child, unless prematurely tainted by being brought up among worldly-minded elders For instance, I have heard grown-up people recall the misery they once suffered from going to school less well dressed than their school-mates; but I can not remember such distresses ever troubling me. I was no more afflicted to see other girls in sashes while I had none than my mother was grieved by the fact that her gowns were of print or muslin when her friends wore silk and satin. I saw she always dressed herself, as she dressed me, neatly, comfortably, as prettily and as much in the fashion as she could afford, and there the matter ended. What we could not afford we neither craved for nor mourned over.

As I grew toward womanhood the great contest between us was who should have the best clothes: I wished it to be the mother, she would rather it had been the daughter. Many a fond battle we had upon this point every time there were new clothes to be bought. I could not bear to see her go on wearing a shabby bonnet and give me a new one, or turn and turn her gowns to the last limits of respectability because I grew out of my frocks so fast that it was almost impossible to keep me well dressed, suitably dressed, which, it was easy to find out, she was most anxious to do.

For I was her only child; and, let me confess the fact, so familiar that I soon ceased to think it of importance, and, indeed, have forgotten when I first discovered it—I was an exceedingly pretty child. Not like herself at all, but the very image of my father. Consequently as I grew up I became not merely pretty, but handsome; beautiful, in short—at fifteen I believe I was downright beautiful—so that there could be no two opinions about me.

Looking in my glass now, I take a pathetic pleasure in recalling this, and my dear mother's pride and delight in the same, which she now and then attempted to hide, though she never tried to deny or conceal the obvious fact of my beauty—first, because it would have been impossible; secondly, because she would have thought it foolish and wrong. She held beauty to be a gift of God, and, as such, to be neither ignored nor despised, but received thankfully, gladly—a real blessing, if regarded and accepted as such in all simplicity and humility.

"Mammy dear," I remember once saying, as I ran into her arms, "am I not a very pretty little girl? Every body says so."

"Yes, my darling, you are a very pretty little girl, and mammy is glad of it; but she is most glad because you are good. Pretty little girls ought always to be exceedingly good."

This lesson she impressed upon me so strongly that I came to think even beauty a secondary thing, and many a comical story was preserved of my answers to my flatterers—children find only too many—"Yes, of course I'm a pretty little girl, but I'm a good girl too." "Mammy says pretty girls are plenty, and good girls scarce; I mean to be a good girl," etc., etc. Simple, silly speeches, no doubt, but they serve to show that I was not vain in any contemptible way. In truth, I was so accustomed to be praised, to look in the glass, and see there a face which could not fail to give myself as much pleasure as it did to my friends, that I believe I accepted my beauty as calmly as people accept most things which they are born to—a title, an estate, or any other accidental appendage of fortune. I rejoiced in it, much as the lilies and roses do, without any ridiculous pride.

My mother rejoiced too—in my eyes, which somebody told her were like a gazelle's; in my hair, purple-black and very long, which she always dressed herself with her own hands till I was a woman grown; in my slender willowy figure—I was tall, like my father, and at thirteen years old had overtopped herself entirely; above all, in a certain well-bred air, which I suppose I always had, for I have overheard people describe me as "a most lady-like child." This quality might have been hereditary, but I myself attribute it to my never having had any companionship except my mother's.

I did not understand then—I do now—why she was so exceedingly particular over my associates; how many and many a little girl whom I wanted to play with I was gently withdrawn from, lest I might catch the tone of that half-and-half "genteel" society which, for a widow of limited income, is not easy to escape. Not until I grew up a woman did I fully comprehend how difficult it must have been for her to make me grow up really a lady, unharmed by the coarse influences of poverty, not always refined poverty, which necessarily surrounded us on every side. She could not have done it, even though we lived as quietly as possible, first in London lodgings, where my father had died, and then in a school, where, in return for my instruction, she took charge of the whole seamstress work of the establishment—she could not possibly have done it, I say, had she not kept me continually by her side, and exposed to no influence except her own.

And *she* was a lady. Aye, even though she was a tradesman's daughter. But the fact that my grandfather, a builder, had been a self-made man, only enough educated to desire to educate his child, did not affect me in the least. My mother's relations, the Dedmans, and my father's, the Picardys, were to me equally mythical. I knew nothing about them, and cared less.

She seldom spoke of either the persons or the incidents of her early life. She seemed to have been drifted out into the world, as Danae was drifted out to sea, with her baby in her arms, utterly uncertain on what shore she would be thrown, or if she would ever touch land at all. But, like Danae and Perseus, we were cast upon a friendly shore. Wherever we went, I remember, every body was kind to us. Perhaps it was the deep instinct of human nature, that inclines people always to be kind to the widow and orphan; but most probably it was my mother's own sweet nature, and her remarkable mixture of gentleness and self-dependence, which made all whom she met ready to help her, because they saw she was willing, to the utmost of her capabilities, to help herself.

I dare say she had her chances of marrying again, but of such a possibility she never dreamed. So we were just "my mother and I," a pair so completely one, and so content in each other, that beyond general kindliness we never cared much for any body outside. We had no visible relations, and not very many friends—intimate friends, I mean, either young or old, who would stand in my place toward her, or in hers toward me. It never struck me to put any playfellow in opposition to my mother; and she often said that ever since I was born she liked my company better than that of any grown-up person.

So we wandered about the world together, changing our mode of life or place of residence as she deemed best both for my health, which was rather delicate, and for my education. It was always me, always for my advantage; of herself and her own pleasure I do not believe she ever thought at all. And therefore her sorrows, whatever they were, brought no bitterness with them. She endured them till they passed by, and then rose out of them to renewed life. She was to the end of her days the happiest-natured woman I ever knew, and the most cheerful of countenance.

Describe her personally I will not—I can not! Who ever could paint a mother's face? It seems, or ought to seem, unlike every other face in the wide world. We have been familiar with it all our lives—from our cradle we have drank it in, so to speak, like mother's milk, and looked up to it as we looked up to the sky, long before we understood what was beyond it — only feeling its beauty and soothing power. My mother's face was like heaven to me, from the time when I lay in her lap, and sucked my thumb, with my eyes steadily fixed on hers, while she told me "a 'tory," until the day when I last stood and gazed down upon it, with its sweet shut mouth and sealed eyes: gazed—myself almost an old woman—wondering that it had suddenly grown so young.

But many, many years, thank God! before that day—years spent in peace and content, and no small share of happiness, since, as I have said, we were always happy merely in being together—occurred that strange time, that troubled six months, to which I have referred, and which even now makes my heart beat with a sensation which no length of time or change of fortunes has ever deadened, nor ever will deaden, until I cease to live. There is no pain in it now—not an atom of pain! no regret, no remorse—but there it is, an unalienable fact, an ineffaceable impression. And it all happened twenty, thirty—no, I will not count how many years ago. I was just seventeen, and my mother was seven-and-forty.

CHAPTER II.

I HAD "finished my education," or was supposed to have done so, though my mother often laughed, and said nobody's education was ever "finished." Still, I had had all the masters that she could afford to give me, and further study was to be carried on by myself. We also left the school, where we had resided so long, in the suburbs of London, and came to live in the country, "all alone by ourselves," as we said. For we two together was the same as being alone, only with the comfort of companionship.

Our abode was a village in Somersetshire, whither we had come chiefly by chance. Like Adam and Eve, "the world was all before us where to choose," and any place seemed pleasant after that horrid "genteel neighborhood," neither town nor country, with the advantages of neither and the unpleasantness of both. At least so I thought in my hasty angry youth, which had such quick eyes to see the dark shades in every picture. But my mother always answered gently that there might have been much worse places than Kilburn, and we had lived very peacefully there for five years. She always saw the sunny side of every thing, rather than the cloudy one. She was of a far more contented disposition than I.

Still it was always I who started new and daring ideas, as I had done in this case. When we decided as to where we should make our new home, I had got out the maps, and proposed laughingly that we should toss up a half-penny, and select the place on which it fell. It fell flat and prone on the town of Bath!

"Bath?—how odd! were you not born there, mother? Of course we'll go and live at Bath."

"Oh, no, no!" she cried, suddenly; then checked herself. "Well, my child, if you wish it particularly, I see no reason why we should not go. There is nobody to go to, certainly; I never had many relations, and those I had are long dead; still, Bath is pretty, oh, so pretty! You never saw any place at all like it, Elma;" and her eyes brightened with a tender sort of memory in them.

"I should be delighted to see it, the home where you lived as a child and a girl—a grown-up girl like me. Also, mother darling, was it not at Bath that you met my father, and were married?"

"Yes."

"Did papa like Bath as much as you?"

"Not quite. He was ill there for many months, you know, and people seldom fancy the place where they are long ill."

"But he fell in love with you there, and that ought to have made him like it."

I had just begun to have an idea that there was such a thing as "falling in love," and that of course it was the happiest thing in all the world.

My mother was silent—so silent that I took her hand caressingly.

"I like sometimes to talk about my father. Was he not very handsome?—And exceedingly like me?"

"You vain little monkey!" smiled my mother.

And then I laughed too at the conceited speech I had unwittingly made. In our harmless fun the slight shadow which had come over my mother's face passed away, and we continued our consultation—we never did any thing without consulting one another—but made no more references to the past. I saw she did not wish it.

Nevertheless, things so happened that, in the first instance, we went from London to Bath just to gratify my curiosity. For three days we wandered about the city—the beautiful lady-city, of which my mother had not said one word too much; but it was too beautiful, too expensive for our small finances. A little dreary, too, despite its beauty. We knew no one—not a soul! and there were so many grand idle people walking about that the place felt far more lonely than London, where every body is busy.

Also—it may seem a foolish, conceited thing to confess, and yet I must, for it is true—these idle people stared at us so, as if they had nothing to do but to stare, and I resented it much. My mother answered my indignation with gentle composure.

"Idle folk will always stare, my child. Besides, you are taller and more remarkable-looking—well, perhaps prettier—than most girls; and then you have such a very little, insignificant mother to walk beside you."

"Nonsense!" I said; for I thought her sweet face and dainty figure the pleasantest to look at in all the world.

"Come, don't let us be cross; let us take the stares patiently, and fancy ourselves the Duchess of Kent and the Princess Victoria, who have to endure the like whenever they go out, as well as the rest of the royal family."

"But I am not one of the royal family."

"No, my child," said my mother, half laughing, half sad; "but Heaven has given you almost as trying a dignity. My poor Elma, people are sure to stare at you wherever you go; but we will avoid it as much as we can. What do you say? Instead of remaining at Bath, which, indeed, we should find far too dear, suppose we were to try and find some pretty, quiet village near it—I remember several—and settle down there, where you will have nobody to look at you but the cows and sheep—except your mother! Will she suffice, my pet?"

"Yes, entirely."

And I spoke the truth. Odd as it may seem, my mother had done wisely in never denying facts as they were. Her fond, candid admiration of me supplied the place of any other; her frank admission of the fact of my beauty—a simple fact, no more—absolutely prevented my having any petty vanity about it. Just as children brought up without any mysteries make none, and those to whom the truth is always spoken can not see the slightest necessity for such a mean trick as lying.

Besides this rather comical reason for our taking flight from Bath, my mother had another, which she did not then tell me. She wished to live in the country—in the healthiest place she could find. I had been studying hard, I was not strong, and the disease of which my father died—last of five brothers—was consumption. My mother had always watched me, I told her sometimes, "as a cat watches a mouse;" but it was not till after-years that I found out the reason.

Still, there was no sign of my father's having left me, with his own strong likeness, this fatal inheritance. My mother had given me not only her moral but her physical qualities—a sound mind in a sound body. The wholesome Dedman blood, the blood of the people, counteracted all that might have been dangerous on my father's side. From that, and from her careful upbringing, I have, though never robust, enjoyed thoroughly good health. No troubles have been able to kill me. I have lived—have been obliged to live—through them all. There have been times when I almost regretted this—when it would have been so much easier to slip from life, and shirk all its duties; when one fell back longingly upon the heathen proverb that "those whom the gods love die young." Not the Christian God! To Him the best sacrifice is not death, but a long, useful, active, healthy life; reaping unto the last Christ's benediction—that it is more blessed to give than to receive, to minister than to be ministered unto.

The nest where my mother and I settled ourselves we found on our very first day of search. It was in a village a few miles from Bath—a small, old-fashioned house in an old-fashioned street, which sloped down in a steep descent to our door. Indeed, the whole neighborhood had a curious up-and-down-iness—very charming to me, who had grown sick of the long level London pavements and suburban roads.

Equally peculiar and attractive was the landlady, true Somersetshire, blunt in words and kind in deeds, who insisted on our accepting from her a lunch of bread and cheese, but declined point-blank to accept us as lodgers. She always had a family throughout the summer, she said—an excellent family from Bath—and she

"'You're a widow. I see?'"

liked to be alone in the winter, and until they came, which was never before June.

But it was now only January, and I had fallen in love with the quaint old house, and its quainter furniture, chiefly of oak, certainly a century old. Also, by a lucky chance, Mrs. Golding had fallen in love with my mother.

Not with me. Oh dear, no! She took the greatest pains to indicate how little she thought of me—considered me a mere chit of a girl, most objectionably pretty.

"I don't care to have good-looking misses about my place. They're always such a bother. If it was only you, ma'am"—and she looked admiringly at my mother's calm face and smooth gray hairs—she had been gray ever since I could remember. "You're a widow, I see?" glancing at the modified form of widow's cap which she always wore.

"Yes, I have been a widow ever since that girl of mine was born."

"And—not over-rich, I suppose, ma'am?"

"No," returned my mother, unoffended; for it never occurred to her to feel the slightest shame or annoyance on account of her poverty.

"Then I think I'll take you. You won't be much trouble. Only your two selves?"

"Only our two selves," said my mother, putting her arm through mine, a good deal amused, but longing, like me, to take refuge in this quiet house, and with one who seemed, though odd, to be a good and kindly woman. "I think, really, you had better take us. You must be rather dull all alone."

"No doubt, ma'am—no doubt. But I couldn't take from you my usual rent—it wouldn't be honest unless the summer-time. Let us see—what shall it be? What would you like to give me?"

My mother laughingly declining to name a sum, this most extraordinary of landladies named one, which, compared with London prices, was perfectly ridiculous, and yet a great relief to our purse. But she declared it was the usual rate of payment for winter lodgings. We agreed, promising to turn out when the summer family arrived.

"But that is five months to come. A great deal may happen in five months," said my mother, half sighing.

"Aye, indeed, ma'am; miss may be married by then; who knows? There is certainly nobody about here to marry her. They're are all old maids in our parts. She won't find one young gentleman, that I can tell her."

I blushed furiously, and felt so insulted that I would almost have walked out of the house on the spot, had not my mother said gently, with that quiet dignity which puts a stop to all possible forwardness,

"We have not begun to think of these things yet, Mrs. Golding. My daughter is only seventeen."

"Well, and I was only seventeen and a half when I married, and a pretty mess I made of it. My face was my fortune, every body said—that was why poor Golding married me; and it didn't last" (no, certainly not, apparently); "and he was an awful worrit, and that did last, and wore me to skin and bone, as you see. Well, well, he's gone now, so we'll say no more about him. Don't you believe in men, miss; don't marry in haste and repent at leisure. That's all I say."

This melancholy sentiment—which the departed Golding, staring down from the wall in red face, blue coat, and yellow waistcoat, did not contradict—amused me so much that it cooled my wrath, and I made no objection to our finally settling the bargain, and agreeing to become Mrs. Golding's inmates on the morrow.

"Only," I said, when we talked over the matter, "we shall have to keep her at a distance, I am sure. She is a very impertinent woman."

"Because she spoke about your marrying, my child? Well, I suppose you will be married some day;" and my mother put back my hair, and looked steadily into my blushing face. "Would you like to be married, Elma? Yes, of course you would. It is a woman's natural destiny. But there is plenty of time—plenty of time."

"I should rather think so."

"And when you do begin to take such a thing into your little head, be sure you tell your mother."

"Of course I shall."

Here we dropped the matter, not unwillingly, I fancy, on either side. It was a topic quite new; at least this was the first time that my mother had named it at all seriously. For me, as a little girl, I had always protested, like most little girls, that I meant to marry my mother; afterward, that I would not marry at all, for fear of having to leave her. Latterly these protestations had ceased, for they seemed to me rather silly; besides, a kind of shyness had crept over me on the subject of love and marriage. Not that I did not think of it; on the contrary, I believe I thought a great deal, but I said nothing. If I could have questioned my mother about her own experience—her own courtship and marriage—it would have opened my heart; but this was almost the only thing upon which she kept silence toward me, or, if I attempted to speak, gently avoided the subject.

She did so now. When I hazarded a question or two apropos of a small house in a back street of Bath, which she showed me in passing, saying she had once lived there for a little while, she answered abruptly; and when we quitted the city—the fair city which I had already begun to be fond of—I think it was rather a relief to her than not.

In a week's time we felt quite settled in our new home. It was such a pretty home, the prettiest we had ever had. The village was such a curious place, with its ancient houses and gardens, shut in by high walls, its picturesque church, and its altogether old-world aspect, as if it had gone to sleep a century ago, and was only half awake still.

We had one favorite walk, called the Tyning—a curious word, the meaning of which I never knew. But the walk was very pleasant: a kind of high path or natural bridge from hill to hill, sloping steeply down on either side. On one hand you saw the distant uplands, on the other the valley below, with a little river winding through it, turning a gray old cloth-mill, which seemed the only manufacturing industry of the place.

One day we crossed the Tyning on our way to an old ruined abbey, which Mrs. Golding said was one of the sights of the neighborhood. It was a bright, clear February day. I threw back my head, and eagerly drank in every breath of the pleasant bracing air. But it made my mother shiver. I placed myself on the windward side of her, and drew her arm through mine, as I had always been in the habit of doing when we walked out, ever since I had discovered, with the pride of thirteen years, that I was half an inch taller than she. She clung to me, I thought, a little closer than usual as we discussed our summer plans.

"We will be idle till March; then we will study regularly. You must not let slip your education. You may need it yet."

She spoke with hesitation, knowing I knew quite well the possibility to which she referred—that she might die prematurely, when her pension would die with her, and mine was too small to maintain me. If I were left motherless, I should also have to earn my bread. But the first terror, if I ever did look at it, blotted the second out of sight entirely.

"If you want me to make use of my education, I will do it," said I, intentionally misapprehending her. "I will turn governess to-morrow, if you wish, though I should hate it—yes, hate it! And you always said it is the last kind of life I am fitted for."

"That is true, my poor child."

I caught her sigh. I saw her sidelong anxious look. Only since I have been gliding down the hill, and watched so many young folks climbing up it, have I recognized fully the meaning of my mother's silent looks—her ceaseless prevision of a future that should last long after hers was ended—if indeed it had not ended long ago, her own individuality being entirely absorbed in this young life of mine. To be a mother is in truth entirely to forget one's self—one's personal interests, griefs, and joys, and to project one's self wholly into the new generation, with its wonderful present, its still more mysterious future, both of which seem apparently to lie in one's own hands. Only apparently, perhaps; and yet we have to act as if it were really so, as if the whole responsibility of her children's lives rested upon the mother. Oh, that all mothers felt it thus! and when they do feel it, oh, if their children could now and then see into their hearts!

I could not into my mother's—not wholly, even though she was so dear to me and I to her. Now and then, as to-day, there seemed something on her mind which I did not understand, something which she tried first to conceal, then to shake off; and finally succeeded.

"No, my darling, I do not wish you to turn governess, or any thing else, just now," said she, gravely. "I only wish you to grow up a well-educated gentlewoman, equal to any position which— But just now your position is to be your mother's own dear, only daughter," added she, suddenly stopping herself; "a sensible, clever—no, not very clever—"

Alas! that was true enough. I was not clever. Nor accomplished, neither; for my wise mother, finding I had little voice and less ear, had stopped my music; my drawing also had come to an end—since, to waste time on any study which requires real talent when one has absolutely none, she considered simply ridiculous.

"No, you are certainly not a genius—you will never set the Thames on fire. But, whatever you are, I am content with you, my daughter."

"Thank you," replied I, humble, and yet proud.

My mother never allowed me to ponder over either

my merits or my short-comings. She said it was better just to do one's work, and not think much about one's self at all. Her satisfaction in me, not often thus plainly expressed — touched and pleased me, and I walked gayly, a weight lifted off my heart. I knew well I was in no sense a brilliant girl. My "face was my fortune," not my brains. This did not matter much now, though there came a time when I would have given half my beauty to possess just a little of what people call "talent." So it is—we generally care most for the qualities which are not ours.

However, just now I cared for nothing and nobody but my mother. She and I strolled on together, enjoying the spring smell in the air, and the colored twilight just beginning to lengthen, and the blackbird's soft love-note—the first of the year—for it was near upon Valentine's Day. Somehow or other we lost our way, and found ourselves not at the ruined abbey, but exactly where we had started; and it was too late to start again.

"Never mind, we will go there some other day" (aye, we did—I have never forgotten *that* day). "Have we not the whole spring before us? And how delicious, mother, to think we have it all to ourselves! No school —no lessons — no visitors. We literally don't know a soul between here and London. Hurrah! How grand it is to have got no friends!"

"But we may make some—I hope we shall."

"I don't. Because they will be falling in love with you and taking you from me; and I like to have you all to myself, mammy!" (Big girl as I was, I often called her "mammy," or "mummy," or "mimi"—some one of the half-hundred pretty names I used to invent for her when I was a baby. But "mother" was my favorite name. Lots of girls had "mammas"—very few had a "mother." None, I averred, like mine.)

She laughed, and told me nobody was likely to dispute my possession. "Especially of such an elderly person as I am growing, for do you know, my child, though the evening is so pleasant, I feel quite tired and cold."

I blamed myself bitterly for having persuaded her to put on a summer cloak—her winter one looked so shabby in the sunshine.

"I protest, mother, you shall not go on a day longer without buying that Paisley shawl we have so long talked about, which will at once be light and warm. We'll go to Bath after it to-morrow."

"Oh no, no!" Again her unaccountable shrinking from this pleasant city, which, as soon as I had left it, I quite longed to see again.

"Well, mother darling, you shall not be vexed; but the shawl must be got somehow, and Bath is the only place to get it at. Will you let me go and buy it all by myself?"

The moment I had made this proposition I was frightened at it, for I had never yet walked a street's length alone; and as to going shopping alone, the idea was dreadful. Yet, as I hurried my mother home, every shiver of hers made my conscience-stings sharper and my resolution more strong.

"I must learn to be useful, and do things sometimes by myself," argued I. "Only trust me! I will try to lose none of the money, and waste it you may be sure I shall not. And when I go into the shop I will not be nervous—not get angry if people do stare at me. Why should not I walk about alone? There is nothing really to be afraid of."

"No, my love; and if you were obliged to do it—if I were away, and you had no protection, I should wish you to do it—brave as a lion, innocent as a lamb. But you are not obliged. Wait a while, and we will choose the shawl together."

But I could not wait—not longer than the few days during which my mother was laid up with severe cold after this unlucky walk. Why had I not taken care that she was warmly clad before I let her buy me that gypsy hat with the checked pink ribbons (how one remembers individually one's girlish clothes—at least, when they are not numerous!) and the brown silk pelisse, which had cost such a deal of money? I hated it—I hated myself. I resolved to have not another new thing all summer, if only I could coax her to be extravagant in the matter of the Paisley shawl. Go to Bath I must—but how?

A bold idea struck me. "Mother, Mrs. Golding is going to Bath to-morrow: may I go with her and buy your shawl? She knows the shop, and will take care of me."

And then, remembering the figure the old woman cut in her enormous bonnet, and cloak of most respectable antiquity, carrying a huge basket, which went full of eggs and returned full of groceries, my mind misgave me. Certainly, to walk up Milsom Street beside Mrs. Golding would require some little moral courage.

I think my mother guessed this, for she smiled.

"Have you considered—"

"Yes, I've considered every thing. What does it matter? I'm not going to be a goose any more."

"But to act on the principle of the man who, walking about in an old coat, said, 'If every body knows me, it's all right; if nobody knows me, it's all right too.' Well done, my child!"

"Then I may go?"

She hesitated; but I was so urgent that at last I got my own way—as I did sometimes now, when it was not actually a wrong way, but simply a question of feeling. I had come to that age, my mother said, when, in many things, she left me to judge for myself.

"Well, I never!" cried Mrs. Golding, when I broached

the subject to her. "Such a fine young lady as you wanting to go to Bath with an old woman like me! And I sha'n't walk either: my old legs can't stand it this muddy weather. I meant to take the carrier's cart."

This was a new perplexity. "But in for a penny, in for a pound." The shawl must be got, and this was the only way to get it. At once, too, that my mother might have it as soon as she was able to go out again.

I smile now to remember, not without a strange sense of fatality, with what passionate persistence I stuck to my point, and carried it. But it was not for myself, it was solely for her—my own dear mother—the centre of all my world.

"We'll go, then, miss, if you can manage to be up in time, for the carrier passes at six in the morning," said Mrs. Golding, rather maliciously. "And when you've been to market with me, I'll go to Pulteney Street or Royal Crescent with you, and look at the fine folks promenading. That is, if you're not ashamed to be seen with an old body who was once as young and bonny as yourself—though I say it."

Mrs. Golding's prehistoric good looks were her weak point, and I did not want to hurt her feelings. The old woman had been very good to us ever since we arrived. So I had no alternative but to consent; and my mother had none but to let me go.

She dressed me, however, in my very simplest and

plainest garments. "It was evident," I told her, "that she wished me to pass for Mrs. Golding's granddaughter."

"That would be difficult," said she. And catching her face in the glass as she looked over my shoulder, fastening my collar behind, I saw her fond, proud smile —wholly a mother's smile. You girls, when you are mothers yourselves, and dress your own daughters, will understand it, and allow that no personal vanity was ever half so pleasant.

"Now, then, turn round, child, and let me arrange your bonnet-strings. How untidy you are!" (Alas, I was—a common failing at seventeen.) "You might with advantage imitate that neat old woman—your supposed grandmother."

"Mrs. Golding? Oh dear! But tell me, what was my real grandmother—your mother—like?"

"I can not remember. You forget I was brought up by my step-mother."

"And my other grandparents on my father's side?"

"I do not know; I never saw them," replied my mother, hastily. "Child, don't forget to buy new ribbons for your hair." It was in long plaits, fastened round my head like a coronet, very pretty to look at—I may say so now.

My mother so evidently disliked the subject that I ventured no other questions. Strangely enough, I had never asked any before, nor thought at all about my remote ancestors. We lived so entirely in the present, and our life, in its mild, monotonous current, was so full, that I never troubled myself about the past. I was not of a very imaginative temperament—besides, the future was every thing to me, as it generally is in our teens.

At this moment up came the carrier's cart. My mother kissed me tenderly—more tenderly than usual, perhaps, it was so seldom I ever had left her for a whole day—put me gayly into that ignominious equipage, and I drove away.

Had she seen, had I seen, that the driver was—not that funny old man in his voluminous capes, but Fate herself, sitting beside him and holding the reins! But no; had I foreknown all, it would have been—with my clear-eyed will it should have been—exactly the same.

"At this moment up came the carrier's cart."

CHAPTER III.

I THOUGHT in my girlhood—I think still—that Bath is one of the most beautiful cities in the world. Florence, they say, is something like it; but I have never seen Florence, and I love Bath, with that fond, half-sad sort of love which hangs about particular places, making them seem to us, all our days, unlike any other places in the wide world.

During our short stay there I had not seen half its beauties, for my mother seemed unwilling to go about more than she was obliged, and it was winter weather; but now as we crept slowly along the high Claverton

Road, and looked down on the valley below, where the river and the canal meandered, side by side, and in and out, glittering in the morning sunshine; then coming suddenly upon it, I saw the white city, terraces, crescents, circuses, streets, one above the other, rising up almost to the top of Lansdowne Hill. I could not help exclaiming, "How beautiful!"

Mrs. Golding, being a Somersetshire woman, looked pleased. She made the carrier stop his jolting cart for a minute or two that I might get a better view.

"Yes, Bath is a nice place, and there's some nice folks in it—to make amends for the nasty ones."

"Who are they?" I inquired.

"Card-players and ball-goers, and worldlings generally," answered Mrs. Golding. "But they're nothing to you, miss, or me either. And there are good folks besides—though they're not many."

I was silent. We had already discovered that Mrs. Golding belonged to a peculiar sect, called Plymouth Brethren, which had lately risen up in the West of England. My mother did not agree with them in their opinions; but she told me that many of them were very good people, and that I must never smile at Mrs. Golding and her extraordinary forms of speech, as if she and her "brethren" were the only children of the Almighty Father, the only receptacles of eternal truth, and accepters of what they called "salvation."

So I forgave her for holding forth a little too harshly on the wickedness of the world, which to me seemed not a wicked world at all, but most beautiful and enjoyable; forgave her, too, for keeping me out of the lively streets — Milsom Street, Gay Street, Quiet Street, such quaint names! Patiently I followed her into the narrow and dirty regions at the bottom of the town, where she transacted her business, selling and buying alternately, but always contriving to keep one eye upon her basket and the other upon me.

Little need was there. Nobody looked at me. In this busy quarter of the city every body was occupied with his or her own affairs. I felt, with some amusement and perhaps a shade of annoyance, that I was being taken for the old woman's granddaughter after all.

Well, what did it matter? Like the Miller of Dee—

> "I cared for nobody, and nobody cared for me,"

except my mother—only and always my mother.

It was very dull going about without her, we were so seldom apart. So as soon as Mrs. Golding had done her business I suggested mine—the shawl, and insisted on getting it at the very best shop in Bath.

Must I confess that, even as an elderly lady, I rather like shopping? Even when I do not buy, the sight of the pretty things pleases me, as it did in the days when I could not afford to buy; when rich silks and dainty muslins were tantalizing impossibilities, and my mother and I looked at them and shook our heads with a resolute smile, but still a smile. What was there to sigh over? We never had to go in rags, or even threadbare, like some people. And when we did enter a shop, money in hand, to clothe ourselves as elegantly and fashionably as we could afford, how we did enjoy it! Much more, I think, than those who have not to pick and choose, but can buy all they fancy without considering the cost. And then our buying had one remarkable feature, which we regarded essential — though I have found since that every body does not so regard it—we always paid.

I took care to let the shopman see my full purse, and was counting my money rather too ostentatiously, and of course awkwardly, when it tumbled down, and one half-sovereign rolled right at the feet of an old gentleman who was just then entering the shop.

He stooped and picked it up, though he was rather infirm, but politeness seemed an instinct with him; then looking round, he offered the coin to me, with a half-smile and a bow.

I bowed too, and said "thank you," rather gratefully, for I thought it a kind thing for an old man to do. But if old, his figure was upright still, and soldierly looking. It made me look at him a second time: my father had been a soldier.

"He offered the coin to me with a half-smile and a bow."

He looked at me, too, not as young men sometimes looked, with rude admiration, but very intently, as if he thought he knew me, and had half a mind to speak to me. But as I did not know him in the least, I quietly turned away, and gave all my mind to the purchase of the shawl.

I have it still, that dear old shawl—old and worn, but pretty still. Often I regard it with a curious feeling, remembering the day I bought it. What a struggle the buying cost me! a battle first against Mrs. Golding, who wanted a bright scarlet centre, whereas this one was white, with a gray "pine-apple" border, and then against myself, for my mother had given me only three pounds, and its price was three guineas, and I had to borrow.

"Yet it is so lovely, so quiet and lady-like, just after my mother's own taste! She would be sure to like it, only she would say it was too dear."

"Not a bit dear: good things are always cheap," said reassuring Mrs. Golding, pressing the three shillings upon me rather boisterously.

To escape—for I saw the old gentleman was watching us and our dispute (probably he had nothing better to do)—I took the money, at which I fancied he smiled.

Perhaps he had heard all that passed: well, what harm? Supposing he did overhear, he could learn nothing except that my mother was poor and careful, with lady-like tastes, and that I liked to please her if possible. Nevertheless, his observant eye vexed me, and I turned my back upon him until we went out of the shop.

However, there was great consolation in thinking of the beautiful shawl. How nice my mother would look in it, and how warm it would be!

"And a real Paisley shawl is never out of fashion," added Mrs. Golding, encouragingly; then drew down the corners of her mouth, saying, "Fashion was a snare."

Very likely; and yet I should have enjoyed being dressed like those young ladies I saw walking up and down Milsom Street in the sunshine. Pleasant as it had been to admire the grand shops in the Corridor and elsewhere, it would have been pleasanter still to be able to go in and buy there whatever I chose. There were scores of pretty things which I longed to take home with me, for myself or my mother, and could only stare at through the tantalizing glass panes. It was a little hard.

Another thing was harder. In spite of Mrs. Golding, who made the fiercest duenna possible, the passers-by did stare at me; idle loungers, who no doubt thought it great fun to inspect a new face, and all the more so because it was under a plain cottage bonnet, and had no protector but an old woman. With a man beside me, a father or a brother, no one would have dared to stare; and if instead of walking I had been driving, it would have been altogether different. Then these young men would have recognized my position, and paid me the same respectful attentions that they offered to other young ladies, to whom I saw them talk and bow, courteous and reverential, while to me—

Was it my lowly condition that exposed me to this rude gaze, or only my beauty? but I hated my beauty since it caused me such humiliation. My cheeks burning, my heart full of angry resentment, I hurried on through the crowded streets, Mrs. Golding trotting after me as fast as she could.

"Where are you going?" she pettishly said at last. "What on earth is the matter with you?"

It was useless to explain, and indeed I hardly knew myself, so I merely replied that I was tired, and proposed that we should go and sit down in the quietest place we could find.

"That will be Marlborough Fields, if you don't mind the cows. People say some of these days there's going to be a grand park made there for the fine folk to walk in, just as they now walk up and down Royal Crescent. You'll want to go and see them? Of course, all you young folk do like the vanities of the world."

Perhaps old folks too; for, though I protested against it, Mrs. Golding, shaking her head in a solemn, incredulous way, took me right into the then fashionable promenade. The high, broad walk in front of the Crescent houses was as full as it could hold of gayly dressed people, walking up and down, and conversing together, for every body seemed to know every body. There were no carriages, but there was a good sprinkling of sedan-chairs, in which the old and infirm went about. Some of them were pitiful spectacles, in their apparent struggle against remorseless age, sickness, decay; their frantic clinging to that poor feeble life, which could no longer be to them either a pleasant or desirable thing.

It made me sad—me to whom, in my strong, fresh youth, life seemed eternal. I looked upon these poor creatures as if their melancholy lot could never concern me, and yet it weighed me down, and I was glad to get out of the crowd into a foot-path leading to the Weston Road. There, in a quiet nook, some kind soul had put up under a shady tree a comfortable seat, where we sat down, and Mrs. Golding took out a huge parcel of provisions: a most ungenteel repast, and I was horrified at it, hungry as I felt; but there was no use in objecting; and, besides, we were quite out of every body's way, the grand people confining themselves entirely to their walk up and down the Crescent, where they could see and be seen properly.

So we sat quiet and alone. Nothing passed us save one carriage—a very fine one—driving slowly toward Weston.

"Bless us!" cried Mrs. Golding, indignantly, "how stuck-up the world is growing! In my time there were only four carriages in Bath, and only the very rich people thought of such a thing."

"Probably the owner of that one is a rich person," said I, carelessly; but I followed it with my eyes, for I was very tired, and I thought how nice it would be to be driving leisurely home instead of waiting about here for an hour, and then being jolted back in that horrid carrier's cart.

These half-sad, half-envious musings must have lasted some minutes, for Mrs. Golding, having eaten and drunk her fill, leaned her head back against the tree in a delicious dose. The same carriage drove past again, and, stopping a little way off, the footman helped out its only occupant, an elderly gentleman, who, after walking feebly a turn or two in the sunshine, came toward the bench, much exhausted, though evidently striving hard against his weakness, and holding himself as upright as he could. Then I perceived he was the same old gentleman who had picked up my half-sovereign for me in the shop.

Glad to return civility for civility, I made room for him, squeezing myself close up to Mrs. Golding—a politeness which he just acknowledged, without looking at me, sat down, quite exhausted, and closed his eyes.

What a contrast it was—the sleepy half-life of these two old people, one on either side of me, with that strong, vivid, youthful life of mine, full of such an endless capacity for pleasure and pain! Would it ever dwindle down to this? Should I ever be like them? It seemed impossible.

Mrs. Golding's eyes were still peacefully shut; but the old gentleman opened his, and, seeing me, gave a start.

"I beg pardon; I am sure I have seen you before—yes, yes, now I recollect. Excuse me." And he took his hat off, clear off, from his reverend white head. "You will pardon an old man for addressing a strange lady; but I really think I must somewhere or other have had the pleasure of meeting you."

I shook my head, smiling.

"Pardon, then, a thousand times. You, young lady, may make a blunder sometimes when you are seventy-three years old."

I said I made blunders now, and I was only seventeen.

"Only seventeen! You look older. But perhaps you are the eldest of a large family?"

"Oh no! We are only two—just my mother and I."

"A most fortunate pair," said he, bowing, but asked no further personal questions. And indeed, though we immediately began talking, and talked straight on, upon all sorts of subjects, for a full half-hour, he never made the slightest approach to any topic that could imply any curiosity about me or my affairs. He was equally reticent about himself, keeping punctiliously to the cautious,

"'You will pardon an old man for addressing a strange lady.'"

neutral ground of pleasant generalities—a characteristic, I often think, of well-bred people, and which constitutes the charm of their society; just as the secret of true politeness consists in one thing—unselfishness; or, as the Bible puts it, "esteeming others better than themselves."

In my short, shut-up life I had seen few men, fewer gentlemen; none, indeed, to compare with the characters in my books—Sir Charles Grandison, the Waverley heroes, and even those of Miss Austin, whom I less approved, for they were so like every body else, and I wanted somebody quite different. Now this old gentleman was certainly different from any one I had ever seen, and I admired him exceedingly.

Nor, recalling him, do I wonder at my admiration, sudden as it was. The fine old head, with its aquiline features, the erect, soldierly bearing, the dignified and yet gentle manners—as courteous to a mere "slip of a girl" as if she had been a duchess—the blandly toned voice, and easy flow of conversation, belonging to the period when conversation was really held as a fine art, and no flippancy or slang was tolerated. I had never seen any one equal to him. Above all, I was struck by his wonderful tact—the faculty of drawing one out, of making one at ease with one's self, so that one unfolded as naturally as a flower in sunshine: which quality, when the old possess, and will take the trouble to use it, makes them to the young the most charming companions in the world.

I was deeply fascinated. I forgot how the time was slipping on, and my mother sitting waiting for me at home, while I was enjoying myself without her, talking to a gentleman whom I had never set eyes on before to-day, and of whose name and circumstances I was as utterly ignorant as he was of mine.

The shadows lengthened, the soft rosy twilight began to fade, and the thrush's long evening note was heard once or twice from a tall tree.

"Spring come again!" said the old gentleman, with a slight sigh. "The days are lengthening already; it is five o'clock," and he looked at his watch, a splendid old-fashioned one, with a large P in diamonds on the back. "My carriage will be up directly. I always dine at six, and dislike being unpunctual, though I have no ladies to attract me homeward, no fair faces to brighten my poor board. Alas! I have neither daughters nor grand-daughters."

A wife, though, he must have had; for there was a thin wedding-ring on the little finger of his left hand, which it fitted exactly, his hands being remarkably small and delicate for such a tall man. I always noticed people's hands, for my mother had told me mine were rather peculiar, being the exact copy of my father's, with long, thin fingers and almond-shaped nails. This old gentleman's were, I fancied, rather like them, at least after the same sort of type.

"You have no granddaughters! What a pity! Would you have liked to have some?"

And then I blushed at this all but rude question, the more so as he started, and a faint color came into his cheek also, old as he was.

"Pardon me: I did not mean exactly that—that— But why should I dilate on my own affairs? She is having a good long doze *al fresco*, this worthy nurse of yours." (Then he at least had not concluded Mrs. Golding to be my grandmother.)

"Yes; I suppose she is tired. We ought to be going home. My mother will be so dull: I have hardly ever left her for a whole day alone."

"Is your mother like you? Or, rather, are you like your mother?"

This was the only question he had put that could at all be considered personal; and he put it very courteously, though examining my face with keen observation the while.

"I, like my mother? Oh no; it is my father I take after. Though I never saw him; I was a baby when he died. But my mother—I only wish I were like her; so good, so sweet, so—every thing! There never was her equal in the whole world."

The old gentleman smiled.

"I dare say she thinks the same of her daughter. It is a way women have. Never mind, my dear; I am not laughing at your happy enthusiasm. It will soon cool down."

"I hope I shall never cool down into not admiring my mother!" said I, indignantly.

"No, of course. Mothers are an admirable institution, much more so than fathers sometimes. But your nurse is waking up. Good-afternoon, madam." He was of the old school, who did not think politeness wasted on any thing in the shape of a woman. "Your young lady and I have been having such a pleasant little conversation!"

"Indeed, sir!" said my duenna, bristling up at once, but smoothing down her ruffled feathers when she perceived it was quite an old gentleman, a real gentleman too, who had been talking to me. "But it's time we were moving home. Are you rested now, Miss Picardy?"

The old man started violently.

"What did you say? What is her name?"

His eagerness, even excitement, put Mrs. Golding on the defensive at once.

"I can't see, sir, that a strange young lady's name is any business of yours. You've never seen her before to-day, and you certainly won't after; so I'm not a-going to answer any of your questions. Come, my dear."

But the old gentleman had fixed his eyes on me, examining me intently, and almost shaking with agitation.

"I beg pardon," he said, turning to Mrs. Golding, with an evident effort; "you are quite right—quite right; but, in this one instance, if you would allow me to know her name—"

"No, I won't; and you ought to be ashamed of yourself for asking it," cried my angry protectress, as she tucked me under her arm, and marched me off; for, of course, resistance on my part would have been ridiculous.

Presently I ventured a remonstrance, but was stopped at once.

"You don't know Bath ways, my dear. Wait till you get home, and then tell your mother."

"Of course I shall tell my mother. But it was a shame to be rude to such a kind old gentleman—the most charming old gentleman I ever saw."

"Very well. Charming or not charming, I've done my duty."

And she hurried me on, till, just stopping to breathe at the corner of Royal Crescent, there overtook us a gray-headed man, who looked like an old family servant. He touched his hat respectfully.

"Beg pardon, but I believe you are the young lady who was sitting beside my master in Marlborough Fields? He desired me to go after you, and give you this card."

Mrs. Golding extended her hand.

"No, no; I was told to give it to the young lady herself. All right. Good-afternoon, miss."

He too looked keenly in my face, and started even as his master had done.

"Lord bless us! The saints be about us!" I heard him mutter to himself.

But he was evidently an old soldier likewise, who simply obeyed orders, asking no questions; so he touched his hat again, and walked back as fast as he could.

I took the card—an ordinary visiting-card—with a name and address printed thereon; a second address, "Royal Crescent, Bath," being hurriedly written in pencil. But the name, when I made it out, caused me to start in intense astonishment. It was—"*Lieutenant-General Picardy.*"

CHAPTER IV.

As was natural, during the whole drive home in that horrid shaky carrier's cart, I thought of little else than the card in my pocket. I had put it there at once, without showing it to Mrs. Golding, who saw I was offended with her, and perhaps recognized that I had some reason to be. But in no case should I have discussed the matter with her. I was very proud in those days, and had no notion of being confidential with my inferiors.

Besides, it might possibly concern us—our own private affairs. The name, Picardy, was such a very peculiar one that this stranger might turn out to be some relative of ours. What relative? Little as I knew about my father, I did know that he had died the last of his race—so it could not be his elder brother. Perhaps an uncle? Or possibly—no, it was too much to expect!—it would be too like a bit out of a book, and a very romantic book indeed—that this most interesting old gentleman should turn out to be my grandfather.

Yet I clung to the fancy, and to a hundred fancies more, until, by the time we reached home, I had worked myself up into a condition of strong excitement.

It was already dark, but I saw my mother's figure against the blind, and her hand put forward to draw it and look out, as she caught the first rattle of the cart wheels down the street. In a minute more I had leaped out, and come face to face with her dear little figure standing at the door, the calm eyes shining upon me—no, shining up at me, for I was so tall—and the cheerful voice saying, in that peculiarly soft tone which rings in my ears even now when I am sad and alone, "Well, my child?"

A sudden thrill went through me. For the first time in my life I knew something which my mother did not know; I had a strong interest in which she possibly might not share. For the Picardy name was hers, but the Picardy blood was wholly mine.

"Well, my child, and have you had a pleasant day?"

I could not answer immediately. She saw, quick as lightning, that things were not all right with me, and perhaps imagining I had been annoyed by some difficulty concerning Mrs. Golding, bade me not tell her a single thing that had happened until I had taken off my bonnet, and had some tea.

"Then you will be rested, and can unfold to me all your adventures."

Adventures, indeed! Little she knew! And some instinct made me put off, minute after minute, telling her the strange thing which had befallen me.

"But you have really enjoyed yourself, my darling," said my mother, anxiously, as she folded up my pelisse, for I was so bewildered that I did less for myself than usual.

"Oh yes, very much. And I have bought your shawl—such a beautiful shawl! Shall we look at it now?"

"Not till after you have had some tea, my child. How tired you look! Are you sure you are quite well?"

"Oh yes! But, mother darling, something has happened—something so strange! Look here: an old gentleman gave me this card—such a charming old gentleman, who sat beside me on a bench and talked to me, and I talked to him. It was not wrong, was it?"

"No, no," said my mother, hurriedly, trying in vain to decipher the card by the dim candle-light.

"And when we left him, he wanted to know my name, and Mrs. Golding was so cross, and refused to give it—so he sent his man after us with this card. Look, is it not strange? It is our name, our very own name, 'Lieutenant-General Picardy.'"

My mother sunk on a chair, deadly pale. "Ah, I knew it would come, some day. My child, my own only child!"

She flung her arms about me, and burst out weeping as I had never seen her weep before.

When she recovered herself I had put the card away, but she asked me for it, and examined it carefully.

"Yes, it must be General Picardy himself. I did not know he lived at Bath; indeed, I doubted if he were living at all. I have not heard of him for so many years."

"But, mother, who is General Picardy?"

"Your grandfather."

I too sank down on a chair, shaking all over with agitation. It was such a surprise. A painful surprise, too, for it implied that my mother had had secrets from me—secrets kept for years.

"And you never told me? Surely I was old enough to know something about my own grandfather, whom I always supposed to be dead."

"I never said so. But still I thought it most probable, since if alive he must have been keeping silence and enmity against me for seventeen years."

"Enmity against you, my own best, dearest mother! Then I will throw his card into the fire, and never think of him again."

She stopped my hand. "No—he is your grandfather, your father's father, and the nearest relation, after me, that you have in the world. Let us talk about him quietly by and by. Come down to tea now, Elma, my child. You know," with a faint struggle at a smile, "you always say, if the world were coming to an end, mother must have her tea." I laughed, and my momentary wrath, first against her, and then against him, passed away. It seems strange, but I was prone to these outbursts of passion when I was a girl, though they never lasted long. They never come now at all. Sometimes I could almost wish they did, if I had my mother there to soothe them.

"And after tea, mother, you will tell me every thing?"

"Yes. I would have told you long ago, but it was a painful story, and one that I thought could not possibly signify to your future, or affect your happiness in any way. Perhaps I judged wrong."

"Oh no, you were right, you always are," cried I, impulsively; and when I heard the story, my reason seconded this conviction.

But first my mother made me tell her my adventure, which I did, concealing nothing, not even my ardent admiration of the old gentleman who was my grandfather—the first real gentleman, I declared, that I had ever seen.

"Yes, I believe he is that," sighed my mother. "So was your father—so were all the family. It is a very old and honorable family."

"I am glad."

Yes; I was glad, and proud also. I looked down on my hands, my pretty hands, then up at my face, where in the old cracked mirror I saw an image—was it not a softened kind of image of that stern old face, with the aquiline nose, firm close mouth, and brilliant eyes? Aye, undoubtedly I was a Picardy.

My mother, if she noticed me, said nothing, but only made me sit down on the hearth-rug at her feet, with my arm across her lap, and her soft hands stroking my hair—our favorite position when we had a talk. Then she began telling me the story of the past.

A sad story, though I could see that she intentionally made it as little so as possible. Still, any body with ordinary perceptions must have felt sure that there had been many painful bits in it, though she glossed them over, and did not dwell upon them.

In the first place, my father's marriage with her had evidently been considered by his father a disgraceful *mésalliance;* for he refused to see him, and would have disinherited him, only the property was entailed. Entailed, however, strictly in the male line, and I was a daughter! My birth, which my father had reckoned on as a means of reconciliation, disappointed him so excessively that he, in his turn, declared he would not look at me, and died a month afterward.

Whether in their brief married life he had been to my mother kind or unkind—whether his own untrueness had brought about its natural results (for he had persuaded her that his father had no objection to their union), whether he came to blame her for having believed in him, to reproach her for having loved him, and loved him, too, when he was an utter wreck in health and fortune—if things were thus or not I can not tell. She did not tell me. She certainly did not praise my father, but she never blamed him; and when I began to blame him she laid her hand on my lips, as if to say that, after all, he was my father.

But my grandfather I was free to criticise if I chose, and I did it pretty sharply too. He, a poor soldier, to insult my mother by accusing her of "catching" my father, when she could get nothing by it, not even money, for the family estate did not fall in till after they were married, and it was *her* father they lived upon—her father, the tradesman, who, however uneducated, had been an honest, independent man, and had educated his child and made her a lady—quite as much a lady as her husband was a gentleman.

So thought I, and said it too, as far as I dared; but my mother always stopped me, and confined herself to strictly relating the facts of the case.

When she was a widow, and my grandfather was living, solitary and childless, at his newly gained estate, she thought there might be some relenting, at any rate toward me; but there was none. Her letter remained long unanswered, and then there came one from the family lawyer, saying that if Miss Picardy—that was myself—were sent to the General at once, she would be received and adopted, on condition that her mother renounced all claim to her, and never saw her again.

"And what did you say?" I exclaimed, in passionate indignation.

"I said that my child was my child—that I would neither renounce her nor connive at her renouncing me so long as I lived. But that after I was dead—and I thought then that my life would be short—she would belong legally to General Picardy, and I would leave orders for her to be sent to him immediately."

"That was wrong."

"No; it was right," returned my mother, slowly and softly. "For my own parents were dead; I had no near kindred, and if I had, General Picardy was as near, or nearer. Besides, though hard to me, I knew him to have been always a just, honorable, upright man—a man to be trusted; and whom else could I trust? I was quite alone in the world, and I might die any day—I often thought I should."

"My darling mother!"

"Yes; it was rather hard to bear," she said, with a quivering lip. "To feel as ill as I often felt then, and to know that my own frail life was the sole barricade my baby had against the harsh world—my poor little helpless baby—my almost more helpless little girl, who was growing up headstrong, self-willed, yet so passionately loving! No wonder I seized upon the only chance I had for your safety after I was gone. I told General Picardy that all I asked of him was to educate you, so as to be able to earn your own living—that he need not even acknowledge you as his granddaughter—his heiress you could not be, for I knew the property passed to a distant cousin. But I entreated him to bring you up so as to be a good woman, an educated woman, and then leave you to fight your own battle, my poor child!"

"But I have had no need to fight it. My mother has fought it for me."

"Yes, so far. Are you satisfied?"

"I should think so, indeed! And now, mother, I shall fight for you."

She smiled, and said "there was no need." Then she explained that having always in view this possibility of my being sent to my grandfather and brought up by him, she had never said a word to me of his unkindness to herself; indeed, she had thought it wisest to keep total silence with regard to him, since if I once began questioning, it would have been so difficult to tell half-truths, and full explanations were impossible to a child.

"But now, Elma, you are no child. You can judge between right and wrong. You can see there is a great difference between avoiding a bad man and keeping a dignified silence toward a good man who unfortunately has misjudged one, under circumstances when one has no power to set one's self right. Understand me, though I have kept aloof from him, I have never hated your grandfather. Nor do I now forbid you to love him."

"Oh, mother, mother!"

I clung to her neck. Simply as she had told her story, as if her own conduct therein had been the most ordinary possible, I must have been blind and stupid not to perceive that it was any thing but ordinary, that very few women would have acted with such wisdom, such self-abnegation, such exceeding generosity.

"You don't blame me, then, child, for keeping you to myself? I was not keeping you to poverty—we had enough to live upon, and, with care, to educate you fit for any position which you might hereafter be called to fill, so that General Picardy need never be ashamed of his granddaughter. For all else, could any thing have made up to my girl for the want of her mother?"

"Nothing—nothing! Oh, what you have gone through, and for me, too!"

"That made it lighter and easier. When you are a mother yourself, you will understand."

"But General Picardy"—for I could not say grandfather—"did he answer your letter?"

"No. Still, I took care he should always have the option of doing so. Wherever we lived, I sent our address to the lawyer. But nothing came of it, so of late years I concluded he was either grown childish—he must be a good age now—or was dead. But I kept faithfully to my promise. I told you nothing about him, and I educated you so as to meet all chances—to be either Miss Picardy, of Broadlands, or Miss Picardy, the daily governess, as I was slowly coming to the conclusion you would have to be. Now—"

My mother looked steadily at me, and I at her. I do not deny the sudden vision of a totally changed life—a life of ease and amusement, able to get and to give away all the luxuries I chose—flashed across my mind's eye. "Miss Picardy, of Broadlands," and Miss Picardy, the poor daily governess. What a difference! My heart beat, my cheeks burned.

"Suppose your grandfather should want you? You said he seemed much agitated at hearing your name; and he must have taken some trouble to inform you of his, and his address too. No doubt he wishes you to write to him."

"I will not. He is a wretch!"

"Hush; he is your grandfather."

"Don't attempt to make excuses for his conduct," cried I, furiously, the more furiously for that momentary longing after better fortunes to which I have pleaded guilty. "I will never forgive him as long as I live."

"That is more than I have ever said of him or any human being."

"Because, mother, you are the most generous woman alive. Also, because the wrong was done to yourself. It is much easier, as you often say, to forgive for one's self than for another person. Myself I don't care for; but I can't forgive him for his behavior to you."

"You ought, I think," was the earnest answer. "Listen, Elma. Unkind as he was, unfairly as he treated me, he himself was treated unfairly too. I could never explain, never put myself right with him. I was obliged to bear it. But it made me tender over him—indeed, rather sorry for him. Never mind me, my child. There is no reason in the world why your grandfather should not be very fond of you."

Here my mother began to tremble, though she tried not to show it, and I felt her grasp tighten over my hand.

"Darling mother," said I, cheerfully, "why should we trouble ourselves any more about this matter? I have seen my grandfather. He has seen me. Let us hope the pleasure was mutual! And there it ends."

"It will not end," said my mother, half to herself. She looked up at me as I stood on the hearth, very proud and erect, I dare say, for I felt proud. I longed to have a chance of facing my grandfather again, and letting him see that I had a spirit equal to his own; that if he disclaimed me, I also was indifferent to him, and wished to have nothing in common with him—except the name, of which he could not deprive me: I too was a Picardy. My mother looked at me keenly, as if I had been another woman's child and not hers. "No, no, it will not end."

But when two, three, four days slipped by and nothing occurred—to be sure, it would have been rather difficult for my grandfather to find us out, but I never thought of that commonplace fact—the sense that all had ended came upon me with a vexatious pain. I had obstinately resisted my mother's proposal to write to General Picardy.

"No; the lawyer has our London address; he can write there, and we shall get it in time. By all means let him have a little trouble in discovering us, as he might have done any time these seventeen years."

"But the address may have got lost," argued my mother. "Or when he comes to think it over, and especially when he gets no answer to his card, he may doubt if you were the right person. Yet, if he only looked at you—"

However, if I bore my father's likeness in my face, I was all my mother in my heart; as self-contained, as independent, only not half so meek, as she. My spirit revolted against my grandfather; bitterly I resented those long years of silence on his part, when, for all he knew, we might have sunk into hopeless poverty, or even starved.

"No, he knew we could not starve," said my mother, when I angrily suggested this. "I told him we had our pension, which doubtless he considered quite enough—for us. You must remember, in his eyes I was a very humble person."

"You, with your education!"

"He never knew I was educated. Nobody ever told him any thing about me," added she, sadly. "He only knew I was a tradesman's daughter; and that, to persons like General Picardy, is a thing unpardonable. His son might as well have married a common servant; he saw no difference; indeed, he said so."

"Oh, mother!"

"It is true—and you will find many others who think so. There are strong class distinctions in the world—only we have lived out of the world; but we can not do so much longer;" and she sighed. "As to ladyhood, an educated woman is every where and always a lady. But you are also a lady born."

And then she told me of my long string of ancestors, and how her marriage must have fallen like a thunderbolt upon the family and its prejudices. Why my father ever risked it, I can not comprehend, except by supposing him to have been a young man who always did what he liked best at the moment, without reflecting on its consequences to himself or to others.

But my mother, my long-suffering, noble-hearted

mother—the scape-goat upon whom all his sins were laid—

> "Has the pearl less whiteness
> Because of its birth?
> Has the violet less brightness
> For growing near earth?"

I repeated these lines to her, half laughing, half crying, vowing that no power on earth should compel me to have any thing to say to General Picardy unless he fully and respectfully recognized my mother.

But there seemed little chance of this heroic resolution being put to the test. Day after day slipped by; the ring of purple and yellow crocuses under our parlor window dropped their cups and lay prone on the ground, to be succeeded by red and lilac primroses. Soon in our daily walks we found the real wild primroses. I brought them home by handfuls, happy as a child. I had never before lived in the country—the real country—such as I had read of in Miss Mitford's and other books; and every day brought me new interests and new pleasures, small indeed, but very delicious.

However, in the midst of all, I think we were both conscious of a certain uneasy suspense—perhaps even disappointment. No word came from my grandfather. Whether we hoped or feared—I hardly knew which my feeling was—that he would find us out, he did not do it. The suspense made me restless, so restless that I was sure my mother saw it, for she proposed to recommence my studies—

> "'Tis better to work than live idle,
> 'Tis better to sing than to grieve,"

said she, smiling.

"But I am not grieving; what should I grieve about? I have every thing in the world to make me happy," was my half-vexed reply.

And yet somehow I was not quite happy. I kept pondering again and again over the story of my parents, and recalling every word and look of my grandfather, who had attracted me to an extent of which I myself was unaware until I began to doubt if I should ever see him any more. Whatever his faults might have been, or whatever faults of others, as my mother half hinted, might have caused them, to me he had appeared altogether charming.

Besides, though I should have been ashamed to own these last, with the thought of him came many foolish dreams—springing out of the Picardy blood, I fancied, and yet before I knew there was any thing remarkable in the Picardy blood they had never come to me—dreams of pride, of position; large houses to live in, beautiful clothes to wear, and endless luxuries both to enjoy and to distribute. Yes, let me do myself this justice—I never wished to enjoy alone.

When we peeped at the handsome old houses walled

in with their lovely gardens, as one often sees in Devonshire villages, or met the inmates, who passed us by, of course, they being the "gentry" of the place, and we only poor people living in lodgings, I used to say to myself, "Never mind, I am as well-born as they; better perhaps, if they only knew it;" and I would carry myself all the loftier because I knew my clothes were so plain and so shabby — for I refused to have any thing that summer, lest my mother should feel compunction about her Paisley shawl.

That lovely shawl! it was my one unalloyed pleasure at this time. She looked so sweet in it—its soft white and gray harmonizing with the black dress she always wore, though she did not pretend to permanent mourning. Though not exactly a pretty woman, she had so much of youth about her still that she gave the effect of prettiness; and being small, slight, and dainty of figure, if you walked behind her you might have taken her for a girl in her teens instead of a woman long past forty. A lady indeed!—she was a lady, every inch of her! The idea of my grandfather supposing she was not! I laughed to myself over and over again as I recalled how I had unconsciously praised her to him. If he expected me to be ashamed of my mother, he would find himself egregiously mistaken.

How did she feel? Was her mind as full as mine of this strange adventure, which had promised so much and resulted in nothing? I could not tell, she never spoke about it; not till, having waited and waited till I could bear it no longer, I put to her the question direct, did she think we should ever hear of my grandfather, and would she be glad or sorry if we never did?

"My child, I hardly know. It may be, as I said, that the lawyer has lost our address, or that General Picardy expects you to pay him the respect of writing first. Would you like to do it?"

"No. And you? You never answered my second question—if we hear of him no more, shall you be sorry or glad?"

My mother hesitated. "At first, I own it was a great shock to know he was so near, and had seen you, because I always felt sure that once seeing you, he would want to have you."

"And would you have let him have me?"

She smiled faintly. "I think I would have tried to do what was right at the time; what was best for you, my darling. But apparently we are neither of us likely to have the chance. I fear you must be content with only your mother."

Only my mother! Did she imagine I was not content? And had her imaginations any foundation?

I think not. The more I recall my old self, that poor Elma Picardy, who had so many faults, the more I feel sure that this fault was not one of them. I had a romantic longing to see my grandfather again, perhaps even a wish to rise to my natural level in society and enjoy its advantages; but love of luxury, position, or desire for personal admiration—these were not my sins. Nothing that my grandfather could have given me would have weighed for a moment in comparison with my mother.

So the weeks went by and nothing happened. It was already the end of April, when something did happen at last.

CHAPTER V.

WE had been taking a long walk, across the Tyning, and down the sloping fields to the deep valley through which the river ran—the pretty river, which first turned an ancient cloth-mill, and then wound out into the open country in picturesque curves. I had a basket with me, and as we sauntered along between the high banks—such a treasure-trove of floral beauty! like most Somersetshire lanes—I filled it with roots of blue and white violets. Even now the smell of white violets makes me remember that day.

When we got into our little parlor, rather tired, both

of us, I set the basket down beside a letter, which I was nearly sweeping off the table. It was not a post letter, but had been sent by hand.

"Stop—what is that?" said my mother.

What was it, indeed? I have it still.

It is a long letter, in a firm, clear, but rather small handwriting; no slovenliness about it, neither the carelessness of youth nor the infirmity of age; a little formal and methodical, perhaps—I afterward learned to like formality and method, at least to see the advantages of both. But the letter:

"Dear Madam,—I write by desire of my cousin, General Picardy, who has for several weeks kept his bed with severe and sudden illness, a sort of suppressed gout, from which he is now gradually recovering. His extremely helpless condition, until at last he sent for me, may account for the long delay in this communication.

"On the day of his seizure, he had accidentally seen and conversed with a young lady whom he afterward had reason to believe was your daughter, and his granddaughter. He asked in vain for her name and address, and then gave his own, on the chance of her being the right person. Receiving no answer, he concluded he had been mistaken. But, unwilling to trust servants with his private affairs, he waited till I could act as his amanuensis, and get from his lawyer the address you once promised always to give. This we have with difficulty obtained.

"It is, of course, a mere chance that the young lady whom the General met, and whose name he fancied was Picardy, should be his granddaughter, but he wishes to try the chance. The bearer of this letter is the old butler who delivered the card, and who declares that the lady to whom he delivered it was the very image of his young master, whom he remembers well.

"Will you, dear madam, oblige me in one thing? Whatever may be your feelings with regard to my cousin, will you remember that he is now an old man, and that any agitation may be dangerous, even fatal to him? One line to say if it was really his granddaughter whom he met, and you will hear from him again immediately. In the sincere hope of this, allow me to sign myself, dear madam, your faithful servant,

"CONRAD PICARDY."

"Conrad Picardy," repeated my mother, aloud. I, reading the letter over her shoulder, was much more agitated by it than she. These weeks of suspense had apparently calmed her, and prepared her for whatever might happen. Her voice was quite steady, and her hand did not shake, as she gave me the letter to read over a second time. "Conrad Picardy. That is certainly the cousin—your grandfather's heir. It is generous of him to try to discover a possible heiress."

"I thought the estate was entailed."

"So it is, the landed estate; but the General can not possibly have lived up to his large income. He is doubtless rich, and free to leave his money to whomsoever he chooses."

"To me, probably?" said I, with a curl of the lip. "Thank you, mother, for the suggestion."

"It would be but a natural and right thing," returned my mother, gently, "though I do not think it very probable. This Conrad has no doubt been like a son to him for years. I remember—yes, I am sure I remember hearing all about him. He was an orphan boy at school; a very good boy."

"I hate good boys!"

Walking to the window, I stood looking out, in the hope that my mother would not notice the excessive agitation which possessed me. Nevertheless I listened with all my ears to the conversation that passed between her and Mrs. Golding.

"No, ma'am, the messenger didn't wait, though he first said he would, and tied his horse to the palings; and I asked him into your parlor, he was such a very respectable-looking man. But the minute I had shut the door he opened it and called me back, to ask whose miniature was that on the chimney-piece—your dear husband's, ma'am. And when I told him that, he said it was quite enough; he would call for an answer to the letter to-morrow morning, for the sooner he got back to Bath the better. And I thought so too, ma'am," in a mysterious whisper; "and do you know I was not sorry to get him out of the house. For I do believe he was the servant of that impertinent old fellow who—"

"Mrs. Golding," I cried, "speak more respectfully, if you please. That 'old fellow,' as you call him, happens to be my grandfather."

If ever a woman was "struck all of a heap," as she would say, it was Mrs. Golding. She had been very kind to us, in a rather patronizing way, as well-to-do commonalty likes to patronize poor gentility—or so I had angrily fancied sometimes; but she had never failed to show us the respect due to "real" ladies. To find us grand folks, or connected with grand folks, after all, was quite too much for her. She put on such an odd look of alarm, deprecation, astonishment, that I burst out laughing.

Much offended, the good woman was quitting the room, when my mother came forward in that sweet, fearless, candid way she had; she often said the plain truth was not only the wisest but the easiest course, and saved people a world of trouble, if they only knew it.

"My daughter is quite in earnest, Mrs. Golding; General Picardy really is her grandfather, and my father-in-law; but, as often happens in families, there has been a long coolness between us, so that when they met they did not recognize one another, until he heard you mention her name. A fortunate chance, and you will not be sorry to think you had a hand in it." (My mother, dear heart! had always the sweetest way of putting things.)

Mrs. Golding cleared up at once. "Indeed, ma'am, I'm delighted. And, of course, he'll be wanting you immediately. I wish you joy. Such a grand carriage, and miss there will look so well in it! A fine old gentleman he was—a real gentleman, as any one could see she was a real lady. Why, ma'am, the day she and I was in Bath, there was not a soul but turned and looked after us, and I'm sure it wasn't at me! You'll make a great show in the world; but don't heed it, don't heed it; it's a poor world after all, Miss Picardy."

Very funny was the struggle between the old woman's pleasure and pride in this romantic adventure, especially since she too had had a finger in the pie, and her acquired habit of mourning over that "world" which she secretly liked still. But we had no time to discuss her and her feelings; we were too full of our own.

"What must be done?" said my mother, as she and I sat down together, the letter before us. "The man said he should call for an answer to-morrow. What shall I say?"

"Whatever you choose, mother dear."

She looked at me keenly. "Have you really no wish, either way? You are old enough to have both a wish and a will of your own."

"Not contrary to yours. You shall decide."

For I felt that if it were left to me, the decision would be so difficult as to be all but impossible.

My mother read the letter over again. "A very good letter, courteous and kind. Let me see; this Conrad was a school-boy, about fifteen or so, when you were born. He would now be between thirty and forty. Probably he is married, with a family to provide for. It is really much against his own interest to help the General to find out a granddaughter."

I laughed scornfully—I was very scornful sometimes in those days. "He may do as he chooses, and so shall I. So, doubtless, will my grandfather, in whose hands we'll leave the matter."

"No—in hands much higher," said my mother, reverently. "Nothing happens by chance. Chance did not bring us here; nor send you, ignorantly, to meet your grandfather in Bath, twice in the same day. It was very curious. Something will come of it, I am sure." (So, in my heart, was I.) "But whatever comes, you will always be my daughter, my one ewe lamb. I have nobody in the world but you."

She held out her arms half-imploringly, as if she

feared she knew not what. As I caressed her, I told her she was a foolish old mother to be so afraid.

"No; I am not afraid. No true mother ever need be. Her little bird may fly away for a time, but is sure to come back to its own safe nest. So will you."

"But I am not going to fly away—not, at least, without you. I never mean to leave you."

"Never is a long word, my darling. Let us content ourselves with settling the affairs of to-day—and to-morrow."

"When we will just send the briefest possible answer —perhaps only your card—to General Picardy; your 'kind compliments and thanks' to Mr. Picardy, this 'good boy' Conrad, and then go a long walk and get more violets."

Alas! I was not quite honest. My thoughts were running upon very different things from violets.

I scarcely slept all night; nor, I think—for I had my head on her shoulder—did my mother sleep much either. But we did not trouble one another with talking. Perhaps both felt by instinct that to talk would be difficult, since, for the first time in our lives, we were looking on the same thing with different eyes, and each had thoughts which she could not readily tell to the other. This was sure to happen one day—it must happen to every human being; we all find ourselves at some point of our lives alone, quite alone. Still, it was rather sad and strange.

Next morning, after breakfast, when my mother had just said, "Now, child, we must make up our minds what to do, and do it at once," there appeared a grand carriage, with two servants, one of them being the same old man who had followed me with his master's card. He presented it once more.

"General Picardy's compliments, and he has sent the carriage, hoping Miss Picardy will come and spend the day with him at Bath. He will send her back in the same way at night."

A brief message, delivered with military exactitude. The one thing in it which struck me was that it was exclusively to Miss Picardy. There was no mention of Mrs. Picardy at all. I wondered, did my mother notice this?

Apparently not. "Would you like to go, my darling?" was all she said; and then, seeing my state of mind, suggested we should go up stairs together. "We will answer the General's message immediately," said she, pointing to a chair in our poor little parlor for the grand servant to sit down.

"Thank you, ma'am," answered he, and touched his forehead, military fashion. Yes; the old soldier at once recognized that she was a lady.

Then we sat together, my mother and I, with our bedroom door shut, hearing the horses champing outside, and knowing that we had only a few minutes in which to make a decision which might alter our whole future lives — my life certainly; and was not mine a part of hers? It had been hitherto — was it possible things would be different now?

"Would you like to go, Elma?—would you be happy in going?"

"In going without you?"

Then she recognized the full import of the message. "I perceive. He does not want me; he wishes you to go alone."

"Then, whatever he wishes, I will not go. Not a step will I stir without my mother. Nobody shall make me do it."

"Stop a minute, my furious little woman. Nobody wants to make you. That is not the question. The question is, how far you are right to refuse a hand held out thus—an old man's hand."

"But if it has struck my mother?"

She smiled. "The blow harmed me not, and it has healed long ago. He did not understand—he did not mean it. Besides, I am not his own flesh and blood—you are. He is your own grandfather."

"But he does not love me, nor I him, and love is the only thing worth having."

"Love might come."

I recall my mother's look as she sat pleading thus, and I wonder how she had the strength to do it. I think there is only one kind of love—mother's love, and that not even the love of all mothers—which could have done it.

She argued with me a long time. At last I begged her to decide for me, just as if I were still a little child; but she said I was old enough to decide for myself, and in such an important step I must decide. All this while the horses kept tramping the ground outside; every sound of their feet seemed to tramp upon my heart. If ever a poor creature felt like being torn in two, it was I at that moment.

For I wanted to go—I longed to go. Not merely for the childish pleasure of driving in a grand carriage to a fine house, but also because I had formed a romantic ideal of my grandfather. I wished to realize it—to see him again, and find out if he really were the kind of man I imagined. If so, how fond of him, how proud of him, I should have been! I, poor Elma Picardy, who never in her life had seen a man—a real, heroic man; only creatures on two legs, with ridiculous clothing and contemptible faces—and manners to match. Not one of them ought to be named in the same day with my grandfather.

Yes, I was thirsting to go to him; but I could not bear to let my mother see it. At last a loop-hole of hope appeared.

"Perhaps there was some mistake in the message

Let us send Mrs. Golding to ask the servant to repeat it."

No; there was no mistake. He was quite sure his master expected Miss Picardy only.

Then I made up my mind. I had a mind and a will, too, when I chose to exercise them; and the thing in this world which most roused me was to see a wrong done to another person. Here the injured person happened to be my own mother. Of course I made up my mind!

"Very well. I will answer the message myself. You, mother darling, shall have nothing to do with it."

And as I spoke I pressed her into an arm-chair, for she looked very pale, and leaning over her, I kissed her fondly. As I did so, it dawned upon me that the time might come, was perhaps coming now, when I might have to take care of my mother, not she of me. Be it so; I was ready.

"Messages are sometimes misdelivered; write yours," said she, looking at me—a little surprised, but I think not sorry; nay, glad.

I took a sheet of paper, and wrote in as clear and steady a hand as I could—

"Elma Picardy thanks her grandfather for his kindness; but, as she told him, she has scarcely ever in her life spent a whole day away from her mother. She can not do it now. She must decline his invitation."

Then I walked down stairs, and gave the letter myself to the servant, the old man who had known my father. He must have seen my father in my face, for he looked at me with swimming eyes — big, beaming Irish eyes (have I ever said that the Picardys were an Irish, or, rather, a French family long Hibernicized?). He held the letter doubtfully.

"Ah, miss, it's to say ye're coming, is it? You that are the young masther's own daughter, and as like him as two peas. The ould masther's mad to see ye. Sure now, ye'll come?"

It was my first welcome among my father's people, and to reject it seemed hard. But I only shook my head.

"No, I'm not coming."

"And why don't ye come, Miss Picardy?" said the old man, with true Irish freedom—the freedom of long devotion to the family. I afterward found that he had dandled on his knee my father and my four dead uncles, and now was nursing his old master with the tenderness of a brother. "Ye're of the ould stock. Wouldn't ye like to visit the General?"

"Very much, but—I could not possibly go without my mother."

The Irish have many faults, but want of tact is not one of them.

"You're right, miss, quite right, and I'll tell the General so if he asks me. Good-day. It'll all come right by and by, mark my words, Miss Picardy."

This was just a little too much. I did not understand people taking liberties with me. I drew myself up, and saw my grandfather's carriage drive away — standing as still as a statue and as proud as Lucifer. But when it was quite out of sight, and my chance gone—perhaps the one chance in my life of rising to the level to which I was born—the pride broke down, the statue melted—I am afraid into actual tears.

My mother should not see them, that I was determined; so I ran into Mrs. Golding's empty kitchen and dried them — although, having left my pocket-handkerchief up stairs, I had to dry them on the round towel! This most unpoetical solution of things knocked all the nonsense out of me, and I went up stairs to my mother with a gay face and a quiet heart.

She had said nothing, one way or other, after she told me to decide for myself; but now that I had decided she looked at me with gladdened eyes, and leaned her head on my shoulder, uttering a sigh of relief. And once again I felt how proud I should be when we had to change places, and I became my mother's shield and comforter, as she had been mine. Sometimes, of course, regrets would come, and wonderings as to how my grandfather had taken my answer; but I put such thoughts back, and after all we had a happy day.

The next day—oh! how lovely it was! I remember it as if it were yesterday. Spring had come at last. The sun shone with the changeful brightness of April and the comfortable warmth of June. The palms were all out, and the scent from their opening buds filled the lanes. The woods were yellow with primroses and blue with violets; hyacinths were not in blossom yet. As for sound, what with larks in the sky, linnets and wrens in the hedge-rows, and blackbirds on every tall tree, the whole world seemed full of birds' singing. A day to make old folk feel young again, and the young—why—I felt alive to the very ends of my fingers with a sense of enjoyment present, a foreboding of infinitely greater delight to come. How can I describe it? the delicious feeling peculiar to one's teens, the "light that never was on sea or shore." No, never was—never could be, perhaps; we only see its dawning. But there may be full day somewhere, beyond this world of pain.

My mother and I were coming home from our long walk. She carried a great bunch of primroses for our parlor; I had a basket of violet roots to plant in Mrs. Golding's garden. I was determined to finish her violet-bed—in spite of my grandfather! indeed, I tried hard to forget him, and to believe that all yesterday had been a dream.

No, it was not a dream, for at that minute we came face to face with a carriage turning round the corner of the solitary Bath road. It was my grandfather's carriage, and he himself sat in it.

That it was he I saw at once, and my mother guessed at once, for she grasped me by the arm. He leaned back, a little paler, a little sterner-looking than I remembered him; but it was not at all a bad face or a mean face. On the contrary, there was something very noble in it; even his worst enemy would have said so. I could have felt sorry for him, as he sat in the sunshine, with his eyes closed, apparently not enjoying this beautiful world at all.

Should we pass him by? That was my first impulse. It would be easy enough; easy also to remain out of doors till all chance of his finding us, if he had really come to call, was over. Pride whispered thus—and yet—

No, it was too late. The old butler or valet, or whatever he was, had seen us; he touched his hat and said something to a gentleman who sat opposite to my grandfather. The carriage stopped, and this gentleman immediately sprang out.

"I beg your pardon; I presume you are Mrs. Picardy?"

He had addressed himself to my mother, taking no notice of me. She bowed; I did nothing; all my attention was fixed on my grandfather, who seemed with difficulty to rouse himself so as to take in what was happening. The other gentleman spoke to him.

"General, this is Mrs. Picardy. Madam, we were going to call. My cousin is too lame to get out of the carriage. Will you mind entering it and driving a little way with him? He wishes much to be introduced to you."

I can not tell how he managed it—the stranger, who, of course, I guessed was not a stranger, but my cousin, Conrad Picardy—however, he did manage it. Almost before we knew where we were, the momentous meeting was over, and that without any tragic emotion on either side. It was just an ordinary introduction of a gentleman to a lady. My mother was calm, my grandfather courteous. The whole thing was as commonplace as possible. No conversation passed—beyond a few words on the extreme beauty of the day and the length of the drive from Bath—until my mother said something about her regret to find the General such an invalid.

"Yes; I suffer much," said he. "Poor old thing!" patting his swathed leg propped on cushions; "it is almost worse than when I was shot in battle. I can not walk a step. I am a nuisance to every body, especially to my good cousin. By the bye, I should have presented him to you—Major Picardy, Mrs. Picardy; and, Conrad, this is my granddaughter, Elma."

He said my name with a tender intonation. It was a family name, my mother had told me; in every generation there had been always at least one Elma Picardy.

"'General, this is Mrs. Picardy.'"

Major Picardy bowed, and then, as my mother held out her hand, he shook hands with us both. His was a touch rather peculiar, unlike all clasps of the hand I ever knew, being at once soft and firm—strong as a man's, gentle as a woman's. I can feel it still, even as I can still see my mother's smile. His face—it seemed as if I had seen it before somewhere—was of the same type as my grandfather's, only not so hard. He looked about thirty-five, or a little older.

"Major Picardy is visiting me now," said my grandfather. "He is kind enough to say he is not weary of my dull house, where, madam, I have nothing to offer you, should you honor me with a visit, but the society of two lonely soldiers."

My mother bowed courteously, acknowledging but not absolutely accepting the invitation.

"Major Picardy is not married, then?" said she, turning to him. "I thought—I imagined— "

"No, not married," said he; and the shadow flitting across his face made my mother speak at once of something else, and caused me to begin weaving no end of romantic reasons why he was still a bachelor, this elderly cousin of mine, for to seventeen thirty-five is quite elderly. But he interested me, being the same sort of man apparently as my grandfather, only younger.

General Picardy was entirely of the old school. He called my mother "madam," and addressed her with the formal politeness of Sir Charles Grandison. In no way did he betray that there had ever been any anger between them, or that he had ever treated her in any way different from now.

Should I condone his offenses? Should I forgive him? Alas! I fear I never once thought of his sins or my condescending pardon. I was wholly absorbed in the pleasure of this meeting, and in my intense admiration of my grandfather.

When the carriage, having moved slowly up and down the village for half an hour, set us down at our own door, he renewed the invitation.

"I will send the carriage for you, madam; and if you will remain the night—a few days—a week—you and this girl of yours—my girl, too" (and he gently touched my hand)—"I shall be only too happy. Fix the day when I may have the honor of receiving you; an early day, I trust."

"Oh, mother," I cried, eagerly, "let us go—let us go to-morrow!"

My grandfather looked pleased.

"See what it is to have a young lady to decide for us elders. Madam, you must agree. Conrad, you will arrange every thing, as far as is possible to us helpless soldiers? Child, if we once let you into our house, I fear you will turn commander-in-chief there, and rule us all."

This speech, implying a future so bright that I hardly dared believe in it, settled the matter. My mother, whatever she felt, betrayed nothing, but assented cheerfully to the plan; and when we all parted it was with the understanding that we should spend the next day and night under my grandfather's roof, "and as many more days and nights, madam, as you may find convenient or agreeable."

CHAPTER VI.

I DID sleep under my grandfather's roof, but it was not for a week after that, and it was without my mother.

That very night she slipped on the stairs, and sprained her ankle—no serious injury, but enough to make her glad to rest on the sofa, and confine herself to our two little rooms.

"And it would never do to go hobbling helplessly about big ones," said she. "Besides, all gentlemen hate invalids—no doubt your grandfather does. He is an old man, and you may have to put up with some peculiarities. I think you will do this better, and get on with him better, quite alone."

"You don't mean me to go alone?"

"Yes, my child," said she, decisively.

And I found she had already answered affirmatively a letter of his—or, rather, of Major Picardy's—begging I might come, and explaining that he had invited a Mrs. Rix, another "elderly" cousin, to stay at Royal Crescent as my companion and chaperon until my mother could join me.

At first I remonstrated vehemently. Either we would

go together, or I would not go at all—at least, not to-morrow, as she had arranged.

"But he earnestly desires it. And you forget, my child, that a man over seventy has not too many to-morrows."

"Oh, you wish me to go? You want to get rid of me?"

My mother smiled—a strangely pathetic smile. In a moment my arms were round her neck.

"I'll do any thing you like, mammy dear—any thing you consider right and best."

"Thank you, my darling. But we will sleep upon it, and see what to-morrow brings."

It brought another urgent letter from my grandfather—that is, his amanuensis—wishing us both to go, in spite of my mother's half-invalid state; but I could not get her to change her mind. Perhaps she was glad of an excuse to stay behind; but chiefly, I fancied, because, thinking always of me, and never of herself, she honestly believed I should get on better with my grandfather alone. Whatever were her reasons, evidently her resolution was taken.

"And now let us pack up, my child; for the carriage" (Major Picardy said it would be sent on chance) "ought to be here directly."

"Put up very few things, mother, for I shall certainly be back in two days," said I, half indignant at her thinking she could do without me so easily.

"You have very few things altogether, my poor Elma; not half what General Picardy's granddaughter ought to wear," said my mother, with one of her troubled looks.

"Nonsense!" and my passionate pride rose up. "He must take me as I am—clothes and all. It is not *his* doing that I have not ran about in rags these seventeen years."

"Hush! my darling. Let by-gones be by-gones. He wishes this, I am sure. If you had seen the way he looked at you the other day! and you are all that is left to him—the only child of his race and name. He is sure to love you."

"Is he?"

Though I said nothing, in my heart of hearts I felt that I too could love my grandfather—if he would let me. There was such a world of love in me then—such a capacity for admiring and adoring people. I longed to find creatures worthy of worship, and to make myself a mat for their feet to walk over. Hopeless delusion! not rare in young girls, but costing them many a pang; yet better and safer than the other delusion, that every body must be admiring and adoring them. After all, I have known worse human beings than poor Elma Picardy at seventeen.

Our preparations were scarcely finished—and I found from the condition of my wardrobe that my mother must have been silently preparing it all the week—when I heard the sound of carriage-wheels. My heart jumped —I could not help it—I was so sorry to go, yet so glad. In truth, I could not understand myself at all.

Major Picardy had said something about fetching me himself; but the carriage was empty. This was a relief; for how could I have talked all the way to Bath with a perfect stranger? A relief also was it that my good-byes had to be so brief. I had no time to think whether I was happy or miserable.

My mother clasped and kissed me fondly, but without tears.

"There is nothing to weep for, my child. Go, and be happy. One only advice I give you—it is your family motto, only put into beautiful Latin—'Do the right, and fear nobody.' Not even your grandfather."

So she sent me away with a jest and a smile—away into the new, beautiful, unknown world! This bright spring day, with the sun shining, the birds singing, the soft southwest wind blowing, what girl in her teens would not have been happy—at least, not very unhappy —even though she had left her mother behind for a few days, and was all alone? I dried my eyes, I sat up in the carriage, and looked about me. Ah, yes, it was indeed a beautiful world!

It is so still; even though my eyes have ceased to shine, and almost to weep; though my heart beats levelly and quietly; and I look behind rather than before, except when I look into the world everlasting. It is—yes, thank God!—it is still to me the same beautiful world.

Leaving the delicious country lanes, we entered Bath streets. There I saw the admired young ladies and the admiring young gentlemen, sauntering idly up and down, looking at one another, and occasionally at me too. I looked at them back again, fearlessly now. Times were changed—my dreams were realized, my pride was healed. As Miss Picardy, seated in her grandfather's carriage, I met the world on an equal footing, and it was very pleasant.

Will any one blame me—I hardly blame myself now—for enjoying things so much, even though I had left my mother? Was it not a delight to her to see me happy? Had she not desired to see me happy? And as I descended from the carriage in front of my grandfather's house at Royal Crescent, I really believe I was one of the happiest girls in the world.

The house stands there yet. I passed it the other day: a group of children were on the steps; a modern carriage, very unlike my grandfather's, waited at the door. New people lived in it, to whom, as to the rest of the world, it seemed just like any other house. But it never will seem so to me. To the end of my days, I could never pass it without turning back to look at it—and remember.

I did not enter it without a welcome. My grandfather was still in his room; but my cousin, Major Picardy, stood at the door, and behind him was an elderly lady, Mrs. Rix, whom I may as well describe, as I did that night in my letter home, as "nothing particular."

Major Picardy I have never described, and I doubt if I can do it now. Other people I see clearly enough; but to me he never seemed like other people. Perhaps, were I to meet him now, for the first time—but no! it would be just the same, I am sure.

The "good boy" had become a good man—that you saw at once by his face—a handsome face, I suppose, since it resembled my grandfather's; but I never remember asking myself whether it were handsome or not. It was *his* face—that was all. He was not a tall man—scarcely taller than I—and his figure was a little bent, being contracted at the chest; but he had great dignity of carriage, and a certain formality of manner, also like my grandfather, which became him as well as it did the General. Both were soldiers, as I have said, and both equally well-born, well-bred, and well-educated.

"Welcome!" he said to me, holding out a kind, warm hand; "welcome, cousin, to the house of all others where you have a right to be welcome. Mrs. Rix, will you take Miss Picardy up to her room?"

Mrs. Rix—who immediately informed me that she was "born a Picardy," and seemed to have an unlimited admiration, mingled with awe, for the whole Picardy race —led the way to the guest-chamber, evidently the best room in the house, which had been prepared for my mother and me. A charming room it was, with its three windows, set in an oval, looking up the smiling hill-side, where, dotted among the green hills, mansion after mansion, and terrace after terrace, were beginning to climb up to the very rim of the deep circular basin in which Bath is built.

"You will find it quite quiet, being at the back of the house. Do you like quiet, my dear?"

I did not know. But I think I liked every thing, and I told my grandfather so when I met him at lunch. He was walking feebly into the dining-room on Major Picardy's arm. At my remark he laughed, and his cousin smiled.

"Away, Conrad, and let Elma see how she likes to be an old man's walking-stick. She is fully as tall as you. Come here, child."

I came, and he leaned on me. Does one love best those who lean upon one? I think some do. From that minute I began, not only to admire, but to love my grandfather.

Was he loving-hearted? It was too much to expect sentiment at his age. This first meal at his table almost choked me, for I was so nervous, so full of conflicting emotions, that it was with difficulty I could keep from

"'Away, Conrad, and let Elma see how she likes to be an old man's walking-stick.'"

crying. But he ate with composure and appetite, talking Bath tittle-tattle to the others, and scarcely noticing me. After lunch he called me to him, and took my face between his soft, withered hands.

"Yes, you are like your father, but still more like your grandmother. A beautiful girl she was; you remember her, Mrs. Rix? and you, Conrad? But no — I forgot. My wife—Lady Charlotte Picardy—has been dead these forty years."

He mentioned the fact quite calmly, not omitting the "Lady" Charlotte. It was odd, I thought, for a man to speak of a dead wife in that tone. Still, he had never married again, but had lived solitary for forty years.

"You will turn her head, General, by comparing her to her beautiful grandmother. And yet it is true," whispered Mrs. Rix, looking at me.

I felt that my other cousin was looking too. He rose.

"Come, where shall we go for our afternoon drive? What have you seen, Miss Picardy?"

"Nothing."

At which, as if I had said something funny, they all smiled at me, these three people, all so much my seniors, to whom I seemed already becoming the child of the house. This fact I felt sure of: their manner to me was so kind. Further, I did not consider—indeed, I was thinking so much about them, that it did not occur to me to trouble myself as to what they thought about me.

Shortly we were out in the sunshine; and, oh, how bright the sunshine is at Bath! and how the white city and green country shine together under it, in soft spring days, such days as this! The carriage moved slowly up the steep hill. Mrs. Rix sat beside the General, Major Picardy and I opposite.

"Take care of his arm," said the ever-fidgety Mrs. Rix, as a jolt in the carriage pushed us together. And then I found out that my cousin was invalided, having been shot in the shoulder at some Indian battle.

"But pray don't look so grave about it," laughed he; "it only makes me a little stiff. I have not much pain now, though the ball is still there. I assure you, I am enjoying my furlough extremely, Miss Picardy."

"Call her Elma—she is still a child," said my grandfather, so affectionately that even the pride of seventeen could not take offense. Besides, was I not a child, and was it not pleasant to be so regarded and so treated by these three kind people?

They seemed different from any people I had ever known, especially the two gentlemen. Both were gentlemen, in the deepest sense of the word. I felt it then by instinct, my reason satisfies me of it now. Both being military men, they had seen a great deal of the world, and seen it with intelligent eyes, so that their conversation was always interesting, often most delightful. Not learned, or I could not have understood it; but this talk of theirs I could understand, and feel happy that I could. To show off one's own cleverness does one harm; but to be able to appreciate the cleverness of other people always does one good.

I was so absorbed in listening that I scarcely looked about me, until the fresh wind of Combe Down blew in our faces, and my grandfather shivered. Major Picardy leaned forward to fasten his cloak for him—it had two lions' heads for a clasp, I remember. Moving seemed to have hurt the wounded shoulder; he turned slightly pale.

"Don't, Conrad. You never think half enough of yourself. Let your arm rest. Here, Mrs. Rix, may I trouble you?"

"Will you not 'trouble' me?"

I said it shyly, with much hesitation, but was rewarded by the sudden bright pleasure in my grandfather's face—and not in his alone. It was curious what pains my cousin took to make me feel at ease, and especially with the General.

When I had fastened the cloak—with rather nervous fingers, I confess—the old soldier took and kissed them, with that "grand seigneur" air which became him so well — then lifted them up. "See, Conrad, a true Picardy hand."

Cousin Conrad (I learned by and by to call him so) smiled. "The General thinks, Cousin Elma, that to be born a Picardy is the greatest blessing that can happen to any human being."

Here Mrs. Rix looked quite frightened, which rather amused me. For I had sense enough to see that the secret of Major Picardy's undoubted influence with the old man was that, unlike most people, he was not afraid of him. This spoke well for both parties. It is only a tyrant who likes having slaves; and as I looked at the General, I felt sure he was no tyrant. Under whatever delusion he had so unkindly treated my mother, was, and is still, a mystery to me, one that I can never penetrate, because the secret of it was doubtless buried in a long-forgotten grave. In all our intercourse he never once spoke to me of his son, my father.

We drove down the steep valley below Combe Down, then reascended and came out upon the beautiful Claverton Road. At Claverton church I exclaimed, "I know this place quite well."

"I thought you knew nothing, and had never been any where. When, my dear, were you here before?"

"The day I first saw you, sir" (I had noticed that Cousin Conrad usually called him "sir," and he had never yet bade me call him "grandfather"), "I drove past here with Mrs. Golding, in the carrier's cart."

"In the carrier's cart! A young lady going about in a carrier's cart!" cried Mrs. Rix, aghast.

"But how courageous of the young lady to own it!"

said Cousin Conrad; and then my grandfather, who had looked annoyed for a moment, brightened up.

"Quite right—quite right. Mrs. Rix, I assure you a Picardy may do any thing. Only, my dear Elma, I hope you will not again patronize your friend the carrier, or indulge in any such eccentric modes of traveling."

"Indeed, young ladies should never do eccentric things," said Mrs. Rix, eying me with a little curiosity, but evidently not having the slightest idea that I was a "poor relation," and ignorant that there had ever been any "difficulties" between my mother and the General. She had lived all her life in India, and was only a very distant cousin; I felt glad she had not been made a confidante of the family history. But Cousin Conrad knew every thing, and I drew courage from his encouraging smile.

"And this was the view you saw from the carrier's cart? Was it a pleasant conveyance?"

"Not very; exceedingly shaky. But I am sure I shall never regret the journey."

"No, I do not believe you ever will," replied Cousin Conrad, suddenly changing into gravity.

We were standing on a tombstone, looking down the valley, he and I only, he having proposed to show me the beautiful little church and church-yard. There we had lingered for ten minutes or more, reading the inscriptions, and stepping from mound to mound—those green mounds which to me implied almost nothing, except a sort of poetic melancholy, which added a tender charm to life—this bright, hopeful young life of mine. But Cousin Conrad was older.

"I am very familiar with graves," he said, stepping round by one of them, not jumping over it as I did. "All belonging to me are dead; my kindred, and the dearest of my friends. I am quite alone in the world."

"Alone in the world! What a terrible thing!"

"I don't feel it so. I have plenty of work to do. My doctor once told me I was not likely to have a very long life, and ever since I have determined to make it as full as possible."

"How?"

"What a puzzling question! especially as just now you see me living the idlest of lives, having nothing in the world to do but to be a little help to your grandfather."

"That is natural. Are you not my grandfather's heir?"

"Another puzzling question. What a catechist you are! Do you mean to interrogate every body like this, when you come out into the world?"

"I can not tell," said I, laughing. "Really, I know nothing of the world. We never lived in it, my mother and I."

"Would you care to live in it?"

"Perhaps. But that would depend upon what my mother wished. She decides every thing."

"Tell me more about your mother."

So I described her, in a few brief passionate words, determined that he at least should fully know all that she really was in herself and all that she had been to me. I can not say what made me do it, or wish to do it, to so slight an acquaintance; but then he never seemed to me a stranger, and he was of my own blood and name.

Also, to speak about my mother seemed to make amends for what was so strange as to appear almost wrong—that I could be happy, actually happy, away from her.

"But I shall not be away long. If she is not able to come here, I shall go back to her, let me see, the day after to-morrow," said I, very decidedly.

"Could you not enjoy staying a while with the General? You like him?"

"Yes," hesitating, but only because I doubted how far I could trust my companion. Then, looking in his face, I felt sure I might trust him. "Yes, I could like my grandfather very much, if only I were certain he would be kind to my mother."

Major Picardy regarded me earnestly. "You may set your mind at rest on that point, now and always."

"Are you sure?"

"Quite sure. He told me so. And when you know him better, you will find him a man who, whatever his other faults may be, is not given to change—perfectly sincere and reliable. And now let us go back. Be as good a girl as ever you can to your grandfather. He wishes for you, and, remember, he needs you."

"Wishes *me?* needs *me?* Oh, I am so glad?"

I went back to the carriage with a heart as light as the lark's that we left singing over the church-yard. My heart sang too, a happy song all to itself, the whole way back. I had found something new in my life—my life which had seemed already as full as it could hold, till these fresh interests came, yet I found it could hold them, and enjoy them too. "I must tell my mother all about it," thought I, and began writing my evening letter in my head. But no words seemed strong enough to express my grandfather's attractiveness and Cousin Conrad's kindness.

The dinner hour was six. Mrs. Rix told me she was going to dress, so I dressed likewise, in my only silk gown—a soft, dark gray—with my best Valenciennes collar and cuffs. I thought my toilet splendid, till I saw Mrs. Rix, in cherry-colored satin, with bare arms and neck, covered only by a black lace shawl. I felt almost like a real "poor relation" beside her, till I met Cousin Conrad's kind smile, as if he understood all about it, and was rather amused than not. Then I forgot my foolish vexation, and smiled too.

As for my grandfather, he took no notice whatever of my clothes, but a good deal of me; talking to me at intervals all dinner-time, and when, that meal being quickly over, a good many people came dropping in, as was the custom in Bath, Mrs. Rix told me, he introduced me punctiliously to every body as "My granddaughter, Miss Picardy."

Some of them looked surprised, and some of them, I was sure, made undertoned comments upon me and my appearance; but I did not care. If my grandfather was satisfied, what did it matter?

The guests were not very interesting, nor could I understand how grown-up people should play with such deep earnestness at those games of cards, which at school, when we made up an occasional round game, I always found so supremely silly—sillier even than building card-houses. But I got a little quiet talk with Cousin Conrad, who, seeing I was dull, came up to me. By and by the evening was over—this first evening, never to be forgotten.

When every body was gone, and we were saying good-night, my grandfather put his hand on my shoulder, and called Mrs. Rix.

"I do not presume to comprehend ladies' costume, but it seems to me that this is a rather 'sad-colored robe,' as

Shakespeare has it, for so young a person. What say you, my dear, would you not prefer to look a little more —more like other young ladies?"

I winced.

"Yes, indeed, General, she ought," said Mrs. Rix. "I have been thinking all the evening, only I did not quite know how to say it, that if Miss Picardy were dressed—as Miss Picardy—that is, if you would allow me to take her to a proper Bath dressmaker—"

But my pride was up. "Thank you; I prefer to wait till my mother comes. It is she who always chooses my clothes."

"As you please. Good-night," said my grandfather, shortly, as he took up his candle and disappeared.

Cousin Conrad gave me a look, a very kind one, yet it seemed to "call me to order," almost like one of my mother's. Was my pride right or wrong? What must I do?

"Follow him," whispered Major Picardy; and I obeyed. I hope it is not a startling confession, but there have been very few people in my life whom I either could or would "obey."

I followed the old man, walking feebly down stairs, and touched him.

"I beg your pardon, I—"

"Pray do not apologize. I merely asked you to give me the pleasure of seeing you dressed as becomes your position—*my* position, I mean—and you declined. It does not matter."

"It does matter, since I have vexed you. I could not help it. Don't you see, sir, that I have got no money? How can I go and buy new clothes?"

He looked puzzled, but a little less severe.

"Why, child, surely you understood that—but it is of no consequence whether I am pleased or not."

"It is of consequence."

"To me, perhaps. I do not flatter myself it can be so to either you or your mother."

Was this speech ironical? Did it infer any ill-feeling toward my mother? If so, I must speak out. I must make him see clearly on what terms we stood.

"Sir," I said, looking him boldly in the face, "I am seventeen years old, and I never saw you, never even heard of you, till a few weeks ago. My mother has brought me up entirely. I am what I am, my mother's child; and I can not be different. Are you ashamed of me?"

He looked, not at me, for he had turned his back upon me, but at my reflection on the mirror opposite—a figure which startled even myself, it stood so tall and proud.

"Ashamed of you? No."

"One word more: do you expect me to be ashamed of my mother?"

Here I felt my hand caught with a warning pressure,

and Cousin Conrad joined us; coming, with his winning smile, right between my grandfather and me.

"Is it not rather too late at night to begin any unnecessary conversation? The whole question lies in a nutshell, Cousin Elma. A young lady from the country comes to visit her grandfather. She is, of course, a little behind the fashion, and as her grandfather wishes her to take the head of his table" (I started at this news), "he naturally wishes her to be dressed according to *la mode* —is not that the word?—like other ladies of her age and station. He has a right to bestow, and she to accept, this or any other kindness. I am sure Mrs. Picardy would approve. Every wise mother knows that it is unwise for any young girl, in any society, to look peculiar."

"Do I look peculiar?"

"Very. Quite unlike any girl I ever saw."

"Is that meant for civility or incivility, Conrad?" said my grandfather, laughing; for, in truth, there was no resisting that charming way Cousin Conrad had of smoothing down people—half in jest, half in earnest. "Then, Elma, we will make you like other girls, if we can, to-morrow. Now, good-night."

A dismissal—decided, though kindly. Evidently my grandfather disliked arguments and "scenes." He preferred the comic to the tragic side of life—in fact, like most men, he could not endure being "bothered"—would do or suffer a great evil to avoid a small annoyance. So

Cousin Conrad that night told me; and so I found out for myself by and by.

At present there was nothing for me to do but to creep up stairs, rather crestfallen, and find Mrs. Rix waiting to conduct me to my room; where she stayed talking a terribly long time, advising me, in elderly and matronly fashion, about the life into which I was about to plunge. She seemed to take it for granted that I was to be a long time in Bath; and she impressed upon me the necessity of doing as other people did, and dressing as other people dressed, and, above all, of trying to please my grandfather.

"For he is an odd man, a very odd man, my dear. I have seen very little of him of late years, but quite enough to find out that. Until he invited me here he never even told me his son had been married, so that to make your acquaintance was a pleasant surprise, Miss Picardy. You must introduce me to Mrs. Picardy. How soon she must have become a widow! And where did she come from? And what was her maiden name?"

"My mother was a Miss Dedman. She was born in Bath," was all I answered to these and several more inquisitive questions.

"And she will be here, I trust, before I leave? Most likely you will both stay with the General for some time? A capital arrangement. He has lots of money to leave, if he has not left it already to Major Picardy, who gets the landed estate. He is very fond of Cousin Conrad; still, he might grow fonder of you, and if he were to alter his will in your favor—"

"I should despise him!"

I stamped with my foot—my tears burst forth; I could not help it—I had been so over-excited that day. And then to be told calmly that I was to stay here in order to worm myself into the old man's good graces, and supplant Cousin Conrad! What a horrid idea! what a humiliating position! I felt inclined to run away that minute, even though it was the middle of the night—run away back to my mother.

The whole thing was so different from what I had been used to. Mrs. Rix, who talked very little before my grandfather and Cousin Conrad, when she talked to me exhibited her true self, so exceedingly small and worldly-minded, that all my pleasant sensations faded out, and I began to feel as if I had got into an atmosphere where I could not breathe properly. When I shut the door upon her, showing her politely out—not much to her regret, for, though I checked them at once, she had been quite frightened at my tears—I threw myself forlornly down upon the bed, and cried like a child for my mother.

CHAPTER VII.

In spite of my protest that if my mother did not come to me, I should go to her directly, two or three weeks slipped by; she did not come, yet I did not go. She kept putting me off from day to day, assuring me that till she could walk well, she was far happier in small rooms than large, and Mrs. Golding was most devoted to her, which I could well believe. Every body loved to serve my mother.

"Besides," she argued, "if your grandfather wishes to keep you, stay. It is your duty, as well as your pleasure, to please him in all possible ways."

Therefore, I found she quite agreed with Cousin Conrad in condemning me for being so proud about accepting kindnesses; she said I ought to wear my new clothes gratefully and gayly, and sent a polite message herself to Mrs. Rix for the care bestowed on my toilet. My dear mother! Not a word of hers expressed or betrayed the slightest pain or jealousy; not a hint ever suggested that, while I was happy and merry, the petted child of the house, for whom every body was planning enjoyments all day long, she was left alone to spend long, dull days, with little to do, and nothing to amuse her, except reading my letters and answering them.

I have all hers, written daily; an extravagance of postage which was made practicable by Cousin Conrad's providing me with no end of franks. They are almost the only letters she ever wrote me, and I read them over still sometimes, with a full heart. A little formal they may be—most people wrote formally in those days—but they are charming letters, with her heart, the mother's heart, at the core of all. She told me every thing, as I her; so that, while our personal separation was hard, there was a strange new delight in reading, as in writing, the visible words of love. Besides, to recount the day's history at night was as good as living it over again.

And what a life it was! even externally; full of endless amusement, with all the attractions of luxury and refinement. I fell into it as naturally as if it had always been mine. "The Picardy blood," I supposed; until Cousin Conrad laughed at me for saying this, and assigning it as a reason for feeling so much at home, as content in a large house as in a small one, with riches as with poverty.

"No," said he, gravely and gently, as if he thought he had hurt me; "the real reason is because poverty and riches are only outside things. The true *you* — Elma Picardy—is the same through both, and unaffected by either."

What did affect me, then? What made me feel as if I saw a new heaven and a new earth, where every body walked up and down like angels? and they were as good as angels, some of them. For me—I never thought if I were good or bad; I did not think much about myself at all. I was happy, but if any body had asked me why, I could not have told. The strangest thing was, my being happy away from my mother; but then *she* was happy too—she assured me of that—and she knew every thing that happened to me, day after day.

It was a curious life, regular even in its dissipation. The only inmates of that large house were my grandfather, Mrs. Rix, and myself. Cousin Conrad lodged in Marlborough Buildings, close by. But he usually met us every morning at the Pump Room, again in the afternoon promenade round Sydney Gardens, or up and down our own Crescent, the most favorite lounge of all. And he always dined with us, he alone generally; for there was little dinner-giving at Bath then, but every body went out of an evening. Besides small parties at private houses, the Assembly Rooms were thronged every night. There were the ordinary balls, beginning at seven and ending at eleven; and the dress balls, which were kept up an hour later, when, as twelve o'clock struck, the master of the ceremonies would hold out his watch to the band; instantly the music stopped, and the dancers disappeared, as if over them hung the doom of Cinderella.

At least so Mrs. Rix told me, for I myself did not go to these balls; my grandfather said I was too young. But I was taken to the dancing practice, where, on stated afternoons, the young gentlemen and ladies for miles round came to the rooms, to be instructed in quadrilles and country dances, and those new round dances, now all the fashion, of which Mrs. Rix much disapproved; I too. The exercise was charming; but to have people's arms round my waist was not pleasant — never could have been, I thought, unless I were dancing with some one very near, and dear, and kind.

On the whole, I liked best the quiet social evenings, at home or abroad, when my grandfather and Mrs. Rix played cards, and I wandered about the room, sometimes alone, sometimes with Cousin Conrad, who, like my grandfather, knew and was known by every body. Though he was not a great talker, and cared neither for cards nor dancing, he was very popular; and so many sought his company that I always felt pleased and grateful when he sought mine.

These evenings always ended at ten o'clock, when we went home, in sedan chairs on wet nights; but when it was fine, we walked back to Royal Crescent, cloaked and hooded, as was the fashion of many ladies. Indeed, one ancient dame used to boast that she often marched, with all her diamonds on, attended only by her maid, the whole way from her house in Norfolk Crescent to the Assembly Rooms.

Mrs. Rix was not brave enough for that; so she and the General had each a chair, Cousin Conrad and I walking after them. How pleasantly the fresh night air used to blow through circus and square; how pretty even the common streets looked, with their lines of lamps; and how grandly solemn was the sky overhead,

> "Thick inlaid with patines of bright gold!"

He used often to say that line to me, with many others, for he was a great lover of Shakespeare and other old writers, of whom I knew almost nothing. Memory fails me a little for modern poetry, but I think I could remember most of that, even now.

We also used to study a little astronomy, which was a

hobby of his, acquired in long night-marches and campings out. I learned all the constellations and their names, and a good deal besides. There was one particular planet, I remember, which night after night used to rise over Beechen Cliff. I called it "my star," at which Major Picardy smiled, and said it was Jupiter, the most prosperous star of any, astrologers believed, and that I should have a most fortunate and happy life. I laughed, and believed it all.

As I soon found out, I was, compared with him, exceedingly ill-educated. This was not my mother's fault, but my own. Beyond exacted lessons, I had never cared to study or to read. Now I felt my own ignorance painfully, horribly. My grandfather had a good library, and one day, when Cousin Conrad found me hunting there, he volunteered to choose some books for me. After that, he used to talk to me about them; and many a time, when the young gentlemen of Bath were whispering nonsense to me — which they did pretty often — I used to grow very weary of them, and keep thinking all the time of what I had been reading that morning, and what Cousin Conrad would say about it when we walked home together at night, under the stars.

Those wondrous stars! those delicious moonlights! that cool, scented, summer dark, perhaps better than either! I was only a girl then—only seventeen. Now I am—no matter what. But to this day, if I chance to walk home of a May night, after a party, the old time comes back again, and the old feeling—the feeling that life was such a grand and beautiful thing, with so much to do, perhaps also to suffer; only suffering looked heroic and sweet—especially if borne for some one else. The bliss of making unheard-of sacrifices for those one loved haunted me continually; indeed, self-martyrdom seemed the utmost joy of existence. For instance, I remember one bleak night silently placing myself as a barrier—oh, what a feeble one!—between a fierce north wind and — a person to whom it was very hurtful to catch cold. I caught cold, of course; but whether I saved that other person is doubtful. No matter. Some people might laugh at me; I have never laughed at myself.

I record these times and these feelings, because many a girl may recognize them as her own experience too. It is nothing to be ashamed of, though it does not always bring happiness. But, I repeat, there are in life more things—possibly better things—than happiness.

When I say I was happy, it was in a way rather different from the calm enjoyment I had with my mother. Little things gave me the keenest joy; other things, equally and ludicrously little, the sharpest pain. For instance, one day, when Mrs. Rix said at table that I was becoming "the belle of Bath," and my grandfather laughed, and Cousin Conrad said—nothing at all! Did he think I liked it? that I cared for being admired and flattered, and talked nonsense to, or for any thing but being loved?—as, it sometimes seemed, they were all beginning to love me at Royal Crescent. Even my grandfather, besides that chivalrous politeness which was his habit toward all women, began to treat me with a personal tenderness very sweet, always ending by saying I was "every inch a Picardy." Which was one of the very few things I did not repeat to my mother.

My darling mother! All this time I had never seen her. Cousin Conrad had. He rode over twice or thrice, bringing me back full news; but though my grandfather said I might have the carriage whenever I liked to go home for a few hours, somehow I never did get it, and was afraid to ask for it. Since, kind as the General was, he always liked to bestow kindnesses, and not to be asked for them.

So time passed. Bath became very hot and relaxing, as is usual in spring; and, either with that or the constant excitement, my strength flagged, my spirits became variable.

"Is she quite well?" I overheard Cousin Conrad asking Mrs. Rix one day; when I answered sharply for myself that I was "perfectly well, only a little tired."

"Of what? Dissipation, or of us all? My child"—he often addressed me so, quite paternally—"would you like to go back to your mother?"

A sudden "stound," whether of joy or pain I knew not, came over me. I paused a minute, and then said, "Yes." Immediately afterward, for no cause at all, I began to cry.

"She certainly is not strong, and ought not to have too much dissipation," said Mrs. Rix, much troubled. "Oh, dear me! and it was only this morning that the General asked me to arrange about taking her to her first public ball."

"Her first ball!"

"My first ball!"

Cousin Conrad and I were equally astonished—whether equally pleased, I could not tell.

"Well, it is natural your grandfather should have changed his mind. I don't wonder that he wishes to see the 'coming out'—is not that what you girls call it?—of the last of his race, to witness the triumph of another 'beautiful Miss Picardy.'"

I looked at him reproachfully. "Cousin Conrad! are you going to talk nonsense too?"

"It is not nonsense. I was merely stating a fact," said he, smiling. "But I beg your pardon."

It is strange how often we think lightly of the gifts we have, and wish for those which Providence has denied. Often, when there was a knot of silly young fellows hovering round me, I thought how much better than being merely pretty would it have been to be clever and accomplished, able to understand the books Cousin Conrad read, and talk with him in his own way. I was so afraid he despised me, and this last remark convinced me of it. My heart sank with shame, and I thought how willingly one would give away all one's beauty—aye, and youth too, only that goes fast enough—to become a sensible, educated woman. Such are really valuable, and valued.

We were all three walking up and down the grassy terrace of a house where my grandfather had come to call, leaving us to amuse ourselves outside, as it was a most beautiful place, centuries old. Every body about Bath knows St. Katherine's Court. As it happens, I have never seen it since that day, but I could remember every bit of its lovely garden—the fountain that trickled from the rocky hill above, the cows feeding in the green valley below, and the tiny gray church on one side.

"I should like to show you the church. It dates long before the Reformation, and is very curious. Will you come, Mrs. Rix, or would you rather sit still here?"

As Major Picardy might have known she would, which I myself did not regret. She was a kind soul, but she never understood in the least the things that we used to talk about, and so she often left us alone. Very dull indeed to her would have been our speculations about the old carved pulpit, and who had preached in it; the yew-trees in the church-yard, which might have furnished bows for the men who fought at Bosworth Field. I tried hard to improve my mind by listening to what Cousin Conrad said. He had such an easy, kind way of giving information, that one took it in, scarcely fancying one was learning at all. Soon I quite forgot my wounded feelings, my fear of his contempt for a poor girl who had nothing in the world to recommend her except her beauty.

Suddenly he turned round and asked me why I had been so vexed with him about the ball. Did I dislike going?

No, I liked it very much.

"Then why were you offended with me? Was it because I called you 'the beautiful Miss Picardy?'"

He had guessed my thoughts, as he often did, just like a magician. I hung my head. "I thought you were laughing at me, or despising me. It is such a contemptible thing to be only pretty. Oh, I wish I could be ugly for a week!"

He smiled. "But only for a week. You would soon be glad to turn back into your old self again, and so would others. Believe me, beauty is always a blessing, and not necessarily harmful. The loveliest woman I ever beheld was also the best."

Who could that be? His mother, or—no, I had never

heard of his having a sister. Still I did not like to ask.

"I would not speak of her to every body," continued he, in a rather hesitating tone, suddenly sitting down. He had a habit of turning pale and sitting down, invalid fashion, though he always refused to be called an invalid. "But I should like to speak of her to you sometimes, for you remind me of her in your height and the color of your hair; though I think — yes, I am quite sure—that on the whole you are less handsome than she. Still, it is the same kind of beauty, and I like to look at it."

He paused, and I sat still, waiting for what was coming next; so still, that a little sparrow came and hopped in at the church door, looked at us, and hopped out again.

"I do not know if you will understand these things, you are still such a child; but, once upon a time, I was engaged to be married."

I started a little. Since my first romantic speculations concerning him — making him the hero of some melancholy history—Cousin Conrad and his marrying had quite gone out of my head. He was just himself—a gentleman of what to me seemed middle age, five-and-thirty probably—always kind and good to me, and to every young lady he knew, but never in the slightest degree "paying attention" to any body. And he had been "engaged to be married." Consequently "in love." (For I had no idea that the two things are not always synonymous.) I felt very strange, but I tried not to show it.

"It was before I went to India," he continued. "I was only three-and-twenty, and she was twenty-one. She had every thing that fortune could give; I too, except perhaps money. But she had that as well; so we did not mind. An honest man, who really loves a woman, and gives her all he has to give, need not mind, though she is rich and he is poor. Do you not think so?"

"Yes."

"One only trouble we had: she was delicate in health. I knew I should always have to take care of her. I did so already, for she had no mother. She was an orphan, and had been a ward of Chancery. The lady who lived with her was a sister of Mrs. Rix."

"Mrs. Rix! She never said a word."

"Oh, no," with a sad kind of smile, "it is so long ago; every body has forgotten, except me. I think I am one of those people who can not forget. Still, I have come to Bath; I have gone over the same walks; I have been to a party at the same house—I mean the house where she lived, and from which she was to have been married."

"*Was* to have been?" asked I, beneath my breath.

"It was only two weeks before the day. We were

both so young and happy—we liked dancing so much—we wanted to have a good dance together in these Assembly Rooms. We had it; and then she would walk home. It was May, but you know how sharp the winds come round street corners here. She caught cold; in a week she died."

Died! So young, so happy, so well beloved! Poor girl! Fortunate girl!

I could not weep for her; something lay heavy on my heart, seemed to freeze up my tears. But I sat quiet, keeping a reverent silence toward a grief which he had thought I could not "understand."

Cousin Conrad had told his story very calmly, letting fall the brief words one by one, in the same mechanical tone; so that any body who did not know him would have thought he felt nothing. What a mistake!

We sat several minutes without speaking; and then, with a sudden impulse of compassion, I touched his hand. He pressed mine warmly.

"Thank you. I thought, Cousin Elma, we should be better friends after this than even before. You will understand that mine has not been an altogether bright life—like yours, for instance; indeed, mine seems half over when yours is scarcely begun. Nor is it likely to be a very long life, the doctors say; so I must put as much into it as I possibly can. As much work, I mean. For happiness—"

"I can see him now, sitting with his hands folded and eyes looking straight before him."

He stopped. I can see him now, sitting with hands folded and eyes looking straight before him — grave, steady, fearless eyes, with a touch of melancholy in them—but nothing either morbid, or bitter, or angry. Such would have been impossible to a nature like his.

"Happiness must take its chance. I neither seek it nor refuse it. Nor have I been, I hope, altogether unhappy hitherto. I have always found plenty to do, besides my profession."

I knew that. It had sometimes made me almost angry to learn, through Mrs. Rix, the endless calls upon him—his health, his time, and his money—by helpless people, who are sure to find out and hang upon a solitary man, who has the character of being unselfish and ready to help every body. When I looked at him, and thought of all that, and of the grief that had fallen upon his life, which, falling upon most men, would have made it a blank life forever, I felt—no, it is not necessary to say what I felt.

There is a quality called hero-worship. It does not exist in every body; and some people say that it is scarcely to be desired, as causing little bliss and much bale; but to those who possess it, and who have found objects whereon to expend it, it is an ecstasy worth any amount of pain.

Though all the world had seemed to swim round me for a minute or two, and Cousin Conrad's quiet voice went through me, word by word, like a sharp knife—still I slowly got right again. I saw the blue sky out through the church door, and heard a lark in the air, singing high up, like an invisible voice—the voice, I could have fancied, of that girl, so long dead, who had been so happy before she died. Happy to an extent and in a sort of way of which the full sweetness had never dawned upon me till now.

To be "in love," as silly people phrase it—to love, as wise and good people have loved, my mother, for instance—I seemed all at once to understand what it was; aye, in spite of Cousin Conrad. And, with that knowledge, to understand something else, which frightened me.

However, I had sense enough to drive *that* back, for the time being, into the inmost recesses of my heart, and to answer him, when, after sitting a minute or two longer, he proposed that we should go back to Mrs. Rix, with my ordinary "Yes." He always laughed at these "Yeses" or "Noes," which he declared formed the staple of my conversation with him or my grandfather. Only, as we went out, I said in a whisper, "Would you mind telling me her name?"

"Agnes."

So we went back to the carriage, and drove home; and I think nobody would have known that any thing had happened.

But little things make great changes sometimes. When I went into the tiny gray church, Mrs. Rix had laughed at the way I bounded down the hilly terrace, called me "such a child!"—no wonder the General thought I was "too young" to go to the Assemblies. When I came out again, I felt quite an old person—old enough to go to twenty balls.

CHAPTER VIII.

THERE came upon me a great craving to see my mother. Not that I wished to tell her any thing—indeed, what had I to tell? In writing about that afternoon at St. Katherine's Court, I merely described the house, the garden, and the old gray church. What had passed therein I thought I had no right—I had certainly no desire—to speak of, not even to my mother; and from the complete silence which followed — Cousin Conrad never referred to it again—it seemed after a day or two almost like a story heard in a dream.

But a dream that never could be forgotten. A young girl seldom does forget the first time she comes face to face with a love story—not in a book, but in real life; meets and sympathizes with those who have actually felt all that she has been mistily thinking about.

Whenever Cousin Conrad looked at me, as he did sometimes, in a very tender, wistful way, as if seeing in my face some reflection of the one long hidden under a coffin-lid, I used to ponder on all he had gone through, wondering how he had ever borne it and lived. But he had lived up to five-and-thirty a useful and honored life;

and though he had hinted it might not be a long one, probably on account of that sad taint in our vaunted Picardy blood—consumption—still there seemed no reason why he should fear or hope—did he hope?—for its ending. Cheerful he was—cheerful, calm, busy; was he also happy? Was it possible he ever could be happy? Endlessly I used to ponder over him and her, and on the brief time of love they had had together; and then, overcome with an unaccountable sadness, I used to turn to thinking of my mother.

If I could only go to her! lay my head on her shoulder, and feel how entirely she loved me—me only out of the whole world. And it seemed as if I had a little neglected her of late, and allowed other people to absorb me too much. Had she guessed this? Did she fancy I loved her less? I would soon show her she was mistaken. As soon as ever my grandfather would allow me, I would go back to the two dear little rooms in our quiet village, and be as merry and happy as if I had never gone away—never known any thing beyond the peaceful life when she and I were all in all to one another. We were so still, only—

Was there any thing in that "only" which made me stop and examine myself sharply? Does there not come a time to the most loving of children when they begin to feel a slight want—when parents and home are not quite sufficient to them? They can no longer lie all day, infant-like, on the mother's breast, and see no heaven beyond her face. Other faces grow pleasant, other interests arise. It seems difficult to content one's self with the calm level of domestic life, with its small daily pleasures and daily pains. They want something larger —grander. They are continually expecting some unknown felicity, or arming themselves against some heroic anguish, so delicious that they almost revel in the prospect of woe.

This state of feeling is natural, and therefore inevitable. If recognized as such, by both parents and children, it harms neither, is met, and passed by.

If I could have gone to my mother! Afterward, the hinderances to this looked so small; at the time they seemed gigantic. First, Mrs. Rix, with her pre-occupation about my toilet and her own at my first ball, which was to happen in a few days. Then my grandfather's dislike to have any thing suggested to him, even to the use of his carriage, except by Cousin Conrad, to whom the whole household were in the habit of applying in all difficulties, who arranged every thing and thought of every body; but he was absent — gone to London on some troublesome law business, somebody else's business, of course.

"I can't tell why," he said, smiling, "except that it is from my being so alone in the world, but I seem fated to be every body's guardian, every body's trustee. Take care; perhaps your grandfather may make me yours, and then what a handful I shall have! and how tightly I shall hold you, like one of the cruel guardians in story-books — especially when you want to marry! No, no, my child, seriously, I will let you marry any body you please."

"Thank you," I said, laughing. He did not know he had hurt me.

We missed him much out of the house, even for a few days. If he had been there, I should easily have got to see my mother. As it was, there seemed no way, except starting to walk the seven miles alone; and I doubted if either she or Cousin Conrad would have approved of that step: it would have seemed so disrespectful to my grandfather.

Thus it came to pass that a fifth week was added to the four, and still I had not seen my mother.

I wished, though, that she could have seen me when I was dressed for the ball; I knew it would have made her happy. That was my consolation for not feeling quite so happy myself when it came to the point, as I supposed all young girls ought to feel on such an occasion. How she would have admired the white silk, festooned with white roses, in which I stood like a statue while Mrs. Rix and her maid dressed me—not half grateful enough, I fear, for their care; for I was thinking of that girl "Agnes," scarcely older than myself, who, probably in some house close by, had once been dressed for one of these very assemblies. So young, so happy; yes, I was sure she had been happy; and I sighed, and my white silk looked dull, and my white roses faded, and that nameless despondency to which the young are so prone fell upon me like a cloud, till Mrs. Rix said, kind soul! "There now; I wish your mother could see you."

The mention of my mother nearly made me burst out crying. Crying when one is dressed for one's first ball! What a strange girl I must have been!

"Come now, my dear, and let your grandfather look at you."

He quite started when I came into his room, regarded me intently, then made me walk to and fro, which I did —as grave and dignified as even he could desire. I was not shy, but rather indifferent, feeling as if it mattered little who looked at me.

"Yes, that will do, Elma; you gratify me much. All the daughters of our house have been noted for their beauty. This generation will be no exception to the rule. I wish I were well enough to witness the *début* to-night of another beautiful Miss Picardy."

I smiled. There was no uncomfortable flattery in my grandfather's grand politeness; it was the mere announcement of a fact. I said nothing. What value was my beauty to me? except that it pleased him—and my mother.

"Yes, you are quite right, General; and I am sure the Major would say the same, if he were here; but I suppose nothing would have persuaded him to accompany us."

"No, Mrs. Rix; you are aware that he has never been to a ball since the death of Miss Frere."

"Oh, poor Miss Frere! How much he was attached to her, and she to him. My sister has told me all about it. A sad story, Miss Picardy, which I will tell you while we are having our tea, if you will remind me."

Which I did not do.

"Elma," said my grandfather, as he sat watching me, looking more benign than I had ever seen him; "you may like to read this before you go."

It was a letter from my mother, by which I found that he had politely urged her coming to see my introduction into society. She excused herself, but promised, if she felt well enough, to pay her long-promised visit "in a few days."

Then I should have my mother, and I need not go away! In a moment my variable spirits rose, and the confused sense of pain which was so new to me slipped away. As I wrapped my beautiful white cloak round me, and caught sight of myself in the mirror on the stairs, I knew I was, on the whole, not unpleasant to look at! and was glad to please even the three women-servants who came to peep at me in the hall.

There was another person entering it, who stopped to look too. He seemed tired with traveling, but in his face was the familiar smile. Kind Cousin Conrad! every body was delighted to see him.

"I am not quite too late, I see. All the world seems collected to behold your splendors, Cousin Elma. May not I?"

He gently put aside my cloak. My heart was beating fast with the surprise of seeing him, but I stood quite still and silent for him to examine my dress and me.

"Thank you," he said, with the slightest possible sigh. "You look very nice. Now let me put you into your chaise." As he did so, he said gently, "Be happy, child. Go and enjoy yourself."

So I did, to a certain extent. How could it be otherwise with a girl of seventeen, who loved dancing with all her heart, and had no end of partners, some of whom danced exceedingly well? Good and bad dancers was the only distinction between them—to me. For all else they might have been automatons spinning round on two legs. Their faces I scarcely looked at. The only face I saw was one which was not there.

How tired Cousin Conrad had looked! Sad too. Had the sight of me in my ball-dress reminded him of old times—of his best-beloved Agnes? All through the whirl of light and music and dancing, I had in my mind's eye the picture of those two as they must have looked, dancing together at their last ball; but I thought of one not wholly with pity, but envy.

Still I danced on—danced with every body that asked me. My feet were light enough, though my heart felt sometimes a little heavy, and I rather wondered why girls thought a ball-room such a paradise; until, crossing through the crowd of figures, all alike either unknown or indifferent to me, I saw one whom I knew. The slight stoop, the head with its short, crisp curls, the grave, quiet eyes, and wondrously beautiful smile, how the sight of him changed all the aspect of the room!

It was very kind of Cousin Conrad to come. This sense of his excessive kindness was my first thought, and then another sense of comfort and enjoyment, such as I used to feel when my mother was by. I could not go to him—I was dancing; but I watched him go to Mrs. Rix, and they both stood watching me, I saw, until they fell into conversation, and did not notice me at all. Then I noticed them.

It is an odd sensation, trying to view as with the eyes of a stranger some one whom you know intimately. Many gentlemen in the room were taller, handsomer, younger than Cousin Conrad; but somehow he was Cousin Conrad, just himself, and different from them all.

I wondered what he and Mrs. Rix were talking about; ordinary things probably: she would not surely be so tactless, so cruel, as to wonder at his coming to-night, or to remind him of the last night he was here, when he danced with Miss Frere as his partner—just as one Sir Thomas Appleton (I had good cause to remember his name afterward) was dancing with me. Oh no! not so. I cared nothing for Sir Thomas Appleton. If I had been dancing with any one I loved, as Agnes loved Cousin Conrad, how different it would have been! Yet he had said I "did not understand."

He was right. I did not understand—not fully. I had no idea whither I was drifting; no more than has a poor little boat, launched on a sunshiny lake without helm or oars, which goes on floating, floating as it can only float, toward the great open sea. There had come a curious change in me, a new interest into my life, a new glory over my world. It was strange, very strange, but the whole room looked different now Cousin Conrad was there.

Imlac, in "Rasselas," says (a trite and often-quoted but most true saying), "Many persons fancy themselves in love, when in reality they are only idle;" and therefore, for all young people, idleness is the thing most to be avoided, since the sham of love, coming prematurely, is of all things the most contemptible and dangerous. But some people never "fall in love" at all; they walk into it blindfold, and then wake suddenly, with wide-open eyes, to find that all the interest of life is concentrated in one person, whom they believe, truly or not, to be the best

"The quadrille over, Sir Thomas Appleton took me to Mrs. Rix, and stood talking with Cousin Conrad."

person they ever knew, and whom they could no more help loving than they could help loving the sun for shining on them, and the air for giving them wherewithal to breathe. This is not being "in love," or being "made love to." It is love, pure and simple, the highest thing, if often the saddest, which a woman's heart can know.

If I had been an angel looking down from the heights of Paradise upon another Elma Picardy, I might have sighed and said, "Poor child!" but I do not know that I should have tried to alter things in any way.

The quadrille over, Sir Thomas Appleton took me to Mrs. Rix, and stood talking with Cousin Conrad, whom he knew; so there was no explanation, save a whisper from Mrs. Rix—

"He says the General sent him. They thought you ought not to be here without some male relative; so he came."

"He is very kind," said I—but I was a little vexed. In those days the one thing that sometimes vexed me in Cousin Conrad was his habit of doing first what he ought and next what he liked to do. I have lived long enough to see that the man who does first what he likes and then what he ought, is of all men, not absolutely wicked, the most hopelessly unreliable.

Cousin Conrad might have come to the ball from duty only, but I think he was not unhappy there. His good heart was strong enough to forget its own sorrows in others' joys. Giving Mrs. Rix his arm, and consigning me to Sir Thomas, he led the way to the tea-room, and made us all sit down to one of those little tables at which people who liked one another's company were accustomed to form a circle to themselves. His pleasant talk brightened us all. Then he proposed taking me round the rooms, and showing me every thing and every body.

"She is so young, with the world all before her," said he to Sir Thomas Appleton. "And it is such a wonderful, enjoyable world."

Aye, it was. As I went along, leaning on Cousin Conrad's arm, and looking at all he showed me, I thought there never was such a beautiful hall. Cinderella's, when the prince was dancing with her, was nothing to it; only, unlike Cinderella, when twelve o'clock struck my white silk did not crumble into rags, my slippers did not drop off from my poor little feet.

"Well, it is over," said I, with a little sigh.

"Yes, it is over," echoed Sir Thomas, with a much bigger one. I had been again his partner, by his own earnest entreaty and Cousin Conrad's desire, that he might be able to tell my grandfather how well I could dance. So I had danced, my very best too, knowing he was looking on, and was pleased with me. It made me pleased with myself, and not vexed, even when I heard people whispering after me, "The beautiful Miss

Picardy." Had not Cousin Conrad said that the most beautiful person he ever knew was also the best?

I wondered if he were thinking of her now. From a certain expression in his face as he stood watching the quadrille, I fancied he was. Yes, he had truly said he was one of those who "can not forget."

I also never forget. Many a ball have I been to in my life, but not one incident of this, my first, has vanished from my memory.

It was over at last, and I felt myself in the midst of a crowd of people pushing toward the door, with Cousin Conrad on one side of me and Mrs. Rix on the other. Sir Thomas Appleton was behind.

"See," said he, "what a beautiful night it is; ever so many are walking home; will you walk home, too, Miss Picardy?"

"No," said Cousin Conrad, decidedly.

He muffled me carefully up, put me in a chair, did the same thing for Mrs. Rix, and then walked off down the street with somebody, I suppose Sir Thomas; but I really never noticed that poor young man. I doubt if I even bade him good-night. In five minutes more he had gone out of my head as completely as if he had never existed.

So much so that when Mrs. Rix came into my room to talk over the ball, and asked me what I thought of him, I answered that I could not tell; I had never thought about him at all.

"Never thought about him! Such a rich, handsome, gentlemanly young man, just come into one of the finest estates in Somersetshire. Well, you are the oddest girl I ever knew."

Was I? How? What could she mean? Surely I had not misbehaved myself, or been uncourteous in any way to this very respectable gentleman? But no; he was Cousin Conrad's friend, and Cousin Conrad had not blamed me in the least, but had met me at the door and parted from me with a kind good-night. He was not displeased with me. Then, whatever Mrs. Rix meant or thought did not matter so very much.

CHAPTER IX.

It was just a week after the ball—a happy week; for, as Mrs. Rix said, all the family seemed happier now Cousin Conrad had come back.

We had missed him much. My grandfather was the sort of man who would be always autocrat absolute in his own house; but Cousin Conrad was his prime minister. To him—the heir presumptive, as every body knew—came every body, with their petitions, their difficulties, their cares. Far and near, all helpless people claimed his help; all idle people his unoccupied time. His money, too. Moderate as his income was, he seemed always to have enough to give to those that needed it. But he invariably gave cautiously, and in general secretly. So much so that I have heard people call Major Picardy a rather "near" man. How little they knew!

We missed him, I say, because he was the guiding spirit of the house. Guiding, for he never attempted to rule. Yet his lightest word was always obeyed, because we saw clearly that when he said, "Do this," he meant, "Do it, not because I say so, but because it is right." The right, followed unswervingly, unhesitatingly, and without an atom of selfishness or fear, was the pivot upon which his whole life turned. Therefore his influence, the divinest form of authority, was absolutely unlimited.

Besides, as Mrs. Rix sometimes said to me — just as if I did not see it all!—he was "so comfortable to live with." In him were none of those variable moods of dullness, melancholy, or ill-temper, which men so often indulge in—moods which in a child we call "naughtiness," and set the sinner in a corner with his face to the wall, or give him a good whipping and let him alone; but in his papa, or grandpapa, or uncle, we submit to as something charmingly inevitable, rather interesting than not, although the whole household is thereby victimized. But Cousin Conrad victimized no one; he was always sweet-tempered, cheerful, calm, and wise. His one great sorrow seemed to have swallowed up all lesser ones, so that the minor vexations of life could not afflict him any more. Or else it was because he, of all men I ever knew, lived the most in himself, and yet out of himself; and therefore was able to see all things with larger, clearer eyes. Whether he knew this or not—whether he was proud or humble, as people count humility, I can not tell. No one could, because he never talked of himself at all.

Young as I was, I had sense to see all this in him, the first man with whom I was ever thrown in friendly relations; to see and—what does one do when one meets that which is perfectly lovable and admirable? admire it? love it? No; love is hardly the word for that kind of feeling. We adore.

This did not strike me as remarkable, because every body in degree did the same. Never was there a person better loved than he. And yet he gave himself no pains to be popular; he seldom tried to please any body particularly; only to be steadily kind and simply good to every body.

Good above all to me, unworthy! Oh, so good!

The one person whose opinion of him I did not know was my mother's, though he had ridden over to see her, taking messages from me, almost every week. But she said little about him, and I did not like to ask. One of the keenest pleasures I looked forward to in this her visit was that she would then learn to know Cousin Conrad as I knew him. Mrs. Rix said, as soon as my mother came to chaperon me, she should go to Cheltenham. Then how happy would we three be, walking, talking together, the best company in the world!

For the first time in my life, I thought without jealousy of my mother's enjoying any body's company but mine. Planning the days to come, which seemed to rise up one after the other, like the slope after slope of sunshiny green which melted into the blue sky at the top of Lansdowne Hill, I sat at my bedroom window, perhaps the happiest girl in all Bath.

Ah, pleasant city of Bath! how sweet it looked to me then, a girl in my teens! How sweet it looks still to me, an old woman! Aye, though I walk its streets with tired feet, thinking of other feet that walk there no more, but in a far-away City which I see not yet; still dear to my heart and fair to my eyes is every nook and corner of that city, where I was so happy when I was young.

Happy, even in such small things as my new dress, which I had been arranging for the evening. We went out so much that I should have been very ill off had not my grandfather given me plenty of beautiful clothes. When I hesitated, Cousin Conrad said, "Take them; it is your right, and it makes him happy." So I took them, and enjoyed them too. It is pleasant to feel that people notice one's dress — people whose opinion one values. I laughed to think my mother would not call me "untidy" now.

Also, I was glad to believe, to be quite sure, that my grandfather was not ashamed of me. When Mrs. Rix told him how many partners I had, he used to smile complacently. "Of course! She is a Miss Picardy—a true Miss Picardy. Isn't she, Conrad?" At which Cousin Conrad would smile too.

He always went out with us now, though he did not dance; but he kept near us, and made every thing easy and pleasant—almost as pleasant as being at home.

But these home evenings were the best, after all. I hoped they would come back again when my mother was here. Often I pictured to myself how we would enjoy them. My grandfather asleep in his chair; my mother and Cousin Conrad sitting on the large sofa, one at either end; and I myself on my favorite little chair, opposite them. How often he laughed at me—such a big, tall girl—for liking such a little chair! They would talk together, and I would sit silent, watching their two faces. Oh, how happy I should be!

I had fallen in so deep a reverie, that when there came a knock to my door I quite started.

It was only Mrs. Rix, coming to say that my grandfather wanted me. But she did it in such a mysterious way—and besides, it was odd that he should want me at that early hour, and in his study, where few ever went except Cousin Conrad.

"What does he want me for? There is nothing the matter?"

"Oh, no, my dear; quite the contrary, I do assure you. But, as I said to the General, 'She is so innocent, I am sure she has not the slightest idea'—oh, dear, what am I saying?—I only promised to tell you that your grandfather wanted you."

"I will come directly."

She said true; I had not the slightest idea. I no more guessed what was coming upon me than if I had been a baby of five years old. I stayed calmly to fold up my dress and put my ribbons by, Mrs. Rix looking on with that air of deferential mysteriousness which had rather vexed me in her of late.

"That is right, my dear. Be very particular in your toilette; it is the proper thing, under—your circumstances. But here I am, letting the cat out of the bag again, which the Major said I was on no account to do."

"Is Cousin Conrad with my grandfather?" said I, with a sudden doubt that this might concern him—his going back to India, or something.

"Oh, no. He and Sir Thomas went away together—Sir Thomas Appleton, you know—who has been sitting with the General these two hours."

"Has he?" and I was just going to add, "How very

tired my grandfather must be!" when I remembered the young man was a favorite with Mrs. Rix; at least, she always contrived to have him near us, and to get me to dance with him. The latter I liked well enough—he was a beautiful dancer; the former I found rather a bore. But then he was an excellent person, Cousin Conrad said, and they two were very good friends; which had inclined me to be kind, kinder than I might otherwise have been, to Sir Thomas Appleton.

Forgetting all about him, I ran down stairs, gayly too. For second thoughts told me there was nothing to be afraid of. If any thing were going to happen—if Cousin Conrad had been returning to India, he would have told me; certainly as soon as he told Mrs. Rix. He had got into a habit of talking to me, and telling me things, very much as a kind elder brother would tell a young sister, whom he wished to make happy with his trust as well as his tenderness. And it did make me happy, more and more so every day. My soul seemed to grow, like a flower in sunshine, and to stretch itself out so as to be able to understand what seemed to me, the more I knew of it, the most perfect character of a man that I had ever heard or read of. And yet he liked me—poor ignorant me! and I was certain, if he were going out to India, or any where else, he would have told me as soon as he told her. So I threw aside all uneasiness, and knocked at my grandfather's door with a heart as light as a child's.

For the last time! It never was a child's heart any more.

"Come in, my dear! Pardon my dressing-gown. If I did not receive you thus early, I might not have caught you at all. You have, I hear, such endless engagements, and are growing the cynosure of every eye in Bath."

"I, sir?" said I, puzzled over the word "cynosure," being, alas! not classically educated, like my grandfather and Cousin Conrad. Still it apparently meant something nice, and my grandfather smiled as if at some pleasant idea; so I smiled too.

"Yes, they tell me you are universally admired," patting my hand affectionately with his soft, old fingers. "Quite natural, too. One of your friends"—he looked at me keenly—"one of your most ardent friends, has been praising you to me for these two hours."

"Sir Thomas Appleton, was it? But he is Mrs. Rix's friend, rather than mine. She is exceedingly fond of him."

I said this, I know I did, with the most perfect simplicity and gravity. My grandfather again looked at me, with a sort of perplexed inquiry, then smiled with his grand air.

"Quite right. The proper thing entirely, in so very young a lady. My dear Elma, your conduct is all I could desire. How old are you?"

"Seventeen and a half."

"My mother, your grandmother—no, she would be your great-grandmother—was, I remember, married at seventeen."

"Was she? That was rather young—too young, my mother would think. She did not marry till she was thirty."

I said that rather confusedly. I always did feel a little confused when people began to talk of these sort of things.

My grandfather drew himself up with dignity.

"Mrs. Picardy's opinion and practice are, of course, of the highest importance. Still, you must allow me to differ from her. In our family, early marriages have always been the rule, and very properly. A young wife is more likely to bend to her husband's ways, and this—especially in cases where the up-bringing has been, hem! a little different—is very desirable. In short, when in such a case a suitable match offers, I think, be the young lady ever so young, her friends have no right to refuse it."

What young lady? Did he mean me? Was any body wanting to marry me? I began to tremble violently—why, I hardly knew.

"Sit down, my dear. Do not be agitated, though a little agitation is of course natural under the circumstances. But did I not say that I am quite satisfied with you? and—let me assure you—with the gentleman likewise."

It was that, then. Somebody was wanting to marry me.

Now, I confess I had of late thought a great deal about love, but of marriage almost nothing. Of course marriage follows love, as daylight dawn; but this wonderful, glorious dawn, coloring all the sleeping world—this was the principal thing. When one sits on a hill-top, watching the sun rise, one does not much trouble one's self about what will happen at noonday. To love, with all one's soul and strength, to spend and be spent for the beloved object; perhaps, if one deserved it, to be loved back again, in an ecstasy of bliss—these were thoughts and dreams not unfamiliar and exquisitely sweet. But the common idea of marriage, as I heard it discussed by girls about me: the gentleman paying attention, proposing, then a grand wedding, with dresses and bridesmaids and breakfast, ending by an elegant house and every thing in good style; this I regarded, if not with indifference, with a sort of sublime contempt. That I should ever marry in that way! I felt myself grow hot all over at the idea.

"Yes, my dear, I assure you Sir Thomas Appleton—"

Now the truth broke upon me! His persistent following of us, Mrs. Rix's encouragement of him, her incessant praising of him to me; and I had been civil and kind to him, bore as he was, for her sake and Cousin Conrad's! Oh me, poor me!

"Sir Thomas Appleton, Elma, has asked my permission to pay his addresses to you. He is a young man of independent fortune, good family, and unblemished character. He may not be—well, I have known cleverer men, but he is quite the gentleman. You will soon reciprocate his affection, I am sure. Come, my dear, allow me to congratulate you." And he dropped on my forehead a light kiss, the first he had ever given me. "Pray be calm. I had wished Mrs. Rix to communicate this fact, but Conrad thought I had better tell you myself."

The "fact," startling as it was, affected me less than this other fact—that Cousin Conrad knew it.

My heart stood still a moment; then began to beat so violently that I could neither hear nor see. Instinctively I shrank back out of my grandfather's sight; but he did not look at me. With his usual delicacy he began turning over papers, till I should recover myself.

For I must recover myself, I knew that, though from what I hardly did know; except that it was not the feeling he attributed to me. Still, I must control it. Cousin Conrad knew all, and would be told all.

When my grandfather turned round, I think he saw the quietest possible face, for he patted my hand approvingly.

"That is right. Look happy—you ought to be happy. Let me again say I am quite satisfied. Sir Thomas has behaved throughout exceedingly like a gentleman. Especially in applying to me first, which he did, he says, by Conrad's advice, you being so very young. But not too young, I trust, to appreciate the compliment paid you, and the great advantage of such a connection. I, for my part, could not have desired for my granddaughter a better marriage; and, let me say it, in choosing you, Sir Thomas will do equal honor to my family and his own."

It never seemed to enter my grandfather's head that I should not marry Sir Thomas Appleton!

What was I to do, a poor, lonely girl? What was I to say when my answer was demanded? "No," it would be, of course; but if I were hard pressed as to *why* I said no—

Easy enough to tell some point-blank lie, any lie that came to hand; but the truth, which I had always been accustomed to tell, without hesitation or consideration, that I could not tell. It burst upon me, while I sat there, blinding and beautiful as sunrise.

Why could I not marry Sir Thomas Appleton or any other man? Because, if so, I should have to give up thinking—as I had lately come to think, in all I did or felt or planned—of a friend I had: who was more to me than any lover in the whole world. A man, the best man I ever knew, who, if twenty lovers were to come and ask me, I should still feel in my heart was superior to them all.

But—could I tell this to my grandfather, or any human being? And if not, why not? What was it, this curious absorption which had taken such entire possession of me? Was it friendship? or—that other feeling which my mother and I had sometimes spoken about, as a thing to come one day? Had it come? And, if so, what then?

A kind of terror came over me. I grew cold as a stone. For my life I could not have spoken a word.

There seemed no necessity to speak. Apparently my grandfather took every thing for granted. He went on informing me in a gentle, courteous, business-like way that Sir Thomas and his sister, "a charming person, and delighted to welcome you into the family, my dear," would dine here to-morrow. "Not to-day; Conrad suggested that you would probably like to be alone with your mother to-day."

That word changed me from stone into flesh again—flesh that could feel, and feel with an infinite capacity of pain! I cried out with a great cry, "Oh, let me go home to my mother."

"I have already sent for her. She ought to be here in an hour," said my grandfather, rather stiffly, and again turned to his papers that I might compose myself.

And I tried, oh, how desperately I tried, to choke down my sobs.

If I could only run away! hide myself any where, anyhow, out of every body's sight! answering no questions and giving no explanations! That was my first thought. My second was less frantic, less cowardly. Whatever happened, I must not go away and leave my grandfather believing in a lie.

Twice, thrice, I opened my lips to speak — just one word — a brief, helpless, almost imploring "No," to be given by him at once to the young man who was so mistaken as to care for me; but it would not come. There I sat like a fool — no, like a poor creature suddenly stunned, who knew not what she said or did — did not recognize herself at all except for a dim consciousness that her only safety lay in total silence.

Suddenly there came a knock at the hall-door close by.

"That's Conrad," said my grandfather, evidently relieved. Young ladies and their love affairs were too much for him after the first ten minutes. "Conrad said he would be back directly. Ah, must you go, my dear?" For I had started up like a hunted hare. At all costs I must escape now, at once too, before Cousin Conrad saw me. "Go, then, pray go. God bless you, my dear."

I just endured that benediction; a politeness rather

than a prayer; and felt my grandfather touch my hand. Then I fled—fled like any poor dumb beast with the hounds after it, and locked myself up in my own room.

I am an old woman now. I very seldom cry for any thing; there is nothing now worth crying for. Still, I have caught myself dropping a harmless tear or two on this paper at the thought of that poor girl, Elma Picardy, in her first moments of anguish, terror, and despair.

It was at first actual despair. Not that of hopeless love; because if it were love, of course it was hopeless. The idea of being loved and married in the ordinary way by the only person whom it would be possible for me to love and marry never entered into my contemplations. The despair was because my mother would be here in an hour, either told, or expecting to be told every thing. And if I did not tell her, she, who knew me so well, would be sure to find it out. What should I do? For the first time in my life I dreaded to look in the face of my own mother.

She must be close at hand now. I took out my watch; ah, that watch! Cousin Conrad had given it me only a week ago, saying he did not want it, it was a lady's watch—his mother's, I think—and it would be useful to me. I might keep it till he asked for it. I did. It goes tick-tick-tick, singing its innocent daily song, just over my heart, to this day. A rather old watch now;

but it will last my time. Laying my forehead on its calm, white face—not my lips, though I longed to kiss it, but was afraid—I sobbed my heart out for a little while.

Then I rose up, washed my face and smoothed my hair, trying to make myself look, externally at least, like the same girl my mother sent away from her, only about six weeks since. Oh, what a gulf lay between that time and this! Oh, why did she ever send me away? Why did I ever come here? And yet—and yet—

No, I said to myself then, and I say now, that if all were to happen over again, I would not have had it different.

So I sat with my hands folded, looking up the same sunny hillside that I had looked at this morning, but the light seemed to have slipped away from it, and was fading, fading fast. Alas! the view had not changed —it was only I.

A full hour—more than an hour—I must have sat there, trying to shut out all thought, and concentrate myself into the one effort of listening for carriage-wheels, which I thought I should hear even at the back of the house. Still they did not come. I had just begun to wonder why, when I heard myself called from the foot of the stairs.

"Is Miss Picardy there? I want Miss Picardy."

The familiar voice, kind and clear! It went through

me like a sword. Then I sprang up and hugged my pain. It was only pain; there was nothing wrong in it; there could not be. Was it a sin, meeting with what was perfectly noble, good, and true? to see it, appreciate it, love it? Yes, I loved him. I was sure of that now. But it was as innocently, as ignorantly, as completely without reference to his loving me, as if he had been an angel from heaven.

Now, when I know what men are, even the best of them—not so very angelic after all—I smile to think how any girl could ever thus think of any man; yet when I remember my angel—not perhaps all I imagined him, but very perfect still—I do not despise myself. He came to me truly as an angel, a messenger, God's messenger of all things pure and high. As such I loved him—and love him still.

"Miss Picardy! Can any one tell me where to find Miss Picardy?"

For the second time I heard him call, and this time it felt like music through the house. I opened my door, and answered over the balustrade—

"I am here, Cousin Conrad. Has my mother come?"

"No."

My first feeling, let me tell the truth, was a horrible sense of relief. Ah me! that I ever should have been glad not to see my mother! Then I grew frightened. What could have kept her from coming? No small reason, surely; if she knew how much I needed her, and why she was sent for. But perhaps no one had told her.

Cousin Conrad seemed to guess at my perplexity and alarm. When I ran down stairs to him, the kind face met me, and the extended hands, just as usual.

"I thought I would give you the news myself, lest you might be uneasy. But there is no cause, I think. Your grandfather only sent a verbal message, and has received the same back, that Mrs. Picardy is "not able" to come to-day, but will write to-morrow. However, if you like, I will ride over at once."

"Oh, no."

"To-morrow, then; but I forget. I have to go to London to-morrow for a week. Would you really wish to hear? I can ride over to-night in the moonlight."

"You are very kind. No."

My tongue "clave to the roof of my mouth"—my poor, idle, innocent, chattering tongue. My eyes never stirred from the ground. Mercifully, I did not blush. I felt all cold and white. And there I stood, like a fool. No, I was not a fool. A fool would never have felt my pain; but would have been quite happy, and gone and married Sir Thomas Appleton.

Did he think I was going to do that? I was sure he was looking at me with keen observation, but he made no remark until he said at last, with a very gentle voice—

"You need not be unhappy, cousin; I think you are sure to see your mother to-morrow."

"Yes."

"Good-by, then, till dinner-time, the last time I shall see you for some days."

"Good-by."

Possibly he thought I did not care about his going, or my mother's coming, or any thing else—except, perhaps, Sir Thomas Appleton.

Without another word he turned away, and went slowly down stairs. It was a slow step, always firm and steady, but without the elasticity of youth. I listened to it, tread after tread, and to the sound of the hall-door shutting after it. Then I went back into my room again, and oh, how I cried!

CHAPTER X.

We had a strangely quiet dinner that evening. There were only we four — my grandfather, Cousin Conrad, Mrs. Rix, and I; and, as usual when we were alone, my grandfather, with courteous formality, took Mrs. Rix in to dinner, and Cousin Conrad took me. I remember, as we crossed the hall, he glanced down on my left hand, which lay on his arm; but he did not pat it, as he sometimes did, and he treated me, I thought, less like a child than he had ever done before.

For me—what shall I say? what can I tell of myself? It is all so long ago, and even at the time I saw every thing through such a mist—half fright, half pain—with a strange gleam of proud happiness shining through the whole.

I believed then, I believe still, that to be loved is a less thing than to love—to see that which is loveworthy, and love it. This kind of attachment being irrespective of self, fears no change, and finds none. If it suffers, its sufferings come to it in a higher and more bearable shape than to smaller and more selfish affections. As Miranda says of Ferdinand—

"To be your fellow
You may deny me, but I'll be your servant,
Whether you will or no."

Aye, and not an unhappy service, though silent, as with a human woman—not a Miranda—it needs must be. I was happy, happier than I could tell, when I had managed that his seat at dinner should be nearest the fire—he loved fires, summer and winter; and that, in the drawing-room, the chair he found easiest for his hurt shoulder to lean against should be in the corner he liked best, where the lamplight did not strike against his eyes. The idea of his wooing or marrying me, or marrying any body, after what he had told me, would have seemed a kind of sacrilege. But it did him no harm to be loved in this innocent way, and it did me good—oh, such infinite good! That quiet dinner-hour beside him, listening to his talk with my grandfather, which he kept up, I noticed, with generous pertinacity, so that nobody might trouble me; the comfort of being simply in the room with him, able to watch his face and hear the tones of his voice—how little can I tell of all this, how much can I remember! And I say again, even for a woman, to love is a better thing than to be loved.

Therefore, girls need not blush or fear, even if, by some hard fortune, they find themselves in as sad a position as I.

When Mrs. Rix fell asleep, as she always did when we

were alone together after dinner, I sat down on the hearth-rug, with her little pet spaniel curled up in my lap, and thought, and thought, till I was nearly bewildered.

Neither she nor any one had named Sir Thomas Appleton. Nobody had taken the slightest notice of what had happened since morning, or what was going to happen to-morrow, except that in Mrs. Rix's manner to me there was a slight shade of added deference, and, in my grandfather's, of tenderness, as if something had made me of more consequence since yesterday. For Cousin Conrad, he was just the same. Of course, to him, nothing that had occurred made any difference.

Sometimes the whole thing seemed like a dream, and then I woke up to the consciousness of how true it all was, and of the necessity for saying and doing something that might end it. For if not, how did I know that I might not be dragged unwittingly into some engagement, some understood agreement that might bind me for life, when I only wanted to be free—free to think, without sin, of one friend—the only man in the world in whom I felt the smallest interest—free to care for him, to help him if he ever needed it—to honor and love him always.

This was all. If I could only get rid of that foolish Sir Thomas, perhaps nobody else would ever want to marry me, and then I could go back into the old ways, externally at least, and nobody would ever guess my secret, not even my mother. For I had lately felt that there was something in me which even she did not understand, a reticence and strength of will which belonged not to the Dedmans, but the Picardys. Often, when I looked into his eyes, I was conscious of being, in character, not so very unlike my grandfather.

Therefore, nobody could force me or persuade me into any marriage—I was sure of that; and sitting in front of the fire—we had fires still, for Cousin Conrad's sake—idly twisting little Flossy's ears, I tried to nerve myself for every thing.

Alas! not against every thing; for when the two gentlemen came in, and behind them a third, it was more than I could bear. To my despair, I began blushing and trembling so much that people might fancy I actually loved him.

But, oh! how I hated him—his handsome face, his nervous, hesitating manner!

"I have to apologize. The General brought me in, just for five minutes, to say how sorry I was not to be able to pay my respects to Mrs. Picardy. To-morrow, perhaps to-morrow—"

"We shall all be most happy to see you to-morrow," said my grandfather, with grave dignity, and, turning to Mrs. Rix, left Sir Thomas to seat himself on a chair by my side.

I suppose I ought to have been grateful. Every girl ought to feel at least gratefully to the man that loves her. But I did not; I disliked, I almost loathed him.

Pardon, excellent, kindly, and very fat baronet, whom I meet every year, when you come up to London with a still handsome Lady Appleton and three charming Miss Appletons, who are all most polite to me — pardon! Every thing is better as it is; both for you and for me.

It was a wretched wooing. Sir Thomas talked nervously to my grandfather, to Cousin Conrad, to every body but me, who sat like a stone, longing to run away, yet afraid to do it. For now and then the General cast on me a look of slight annoyance — if so courteous a gentleman could ever look annoyed; and Mrs. Rix came and whispered to me not to be "frightened." Frightened, indeed! At what? At a creature who was more than indifferent — absolutely detestable — to me, from the topmost curl of his black hair to the sole of his shining boots. He must have seen this; I wanted him to see it. Yet still he stayed on, and on, as if he would never go.

When at last he did, and I faced the three with whom I had lived so happily all these weeks—the three who knew every thing, and knew that I knew they knew it —it was a dreadful moment.

"I think we had better retire," said my grandfather, rather sternly. "Conrad, I want you for a few minutes.

And Mrs. Rix, you who are accustomed to the ways of society, will perhaps take the trouble to explain to my granddaughter that—that—"

"I understand, General. Rely upon me," said Mrs. Rix, mysteriously.

And then, with the briefest good-night to me, my grandfather left the room.

Mrs. Rix, having her tongue now unsealed, made the most of her opportunity. How she did talk! What about, I very dimly remember, except that it was on the great advantage of being married young, and to a person of wealth and standing. Then she held out to me all the blessings that would come to me on my marriage—country house, town house, carriages, horses, dresses, diamonds—the Appleton diamonds were known all over the county. In short, she painted my future *couleur de rose*, only it seemed mere landscape-painting, figures omitted, especially one figure which I had heretofore considered most important of all—the husband.

What did I answer? Nothing—I had nothing to say. To speak to the poor woman would have been like two people talking in different languages. Besides, I despised too much all her arguments, herself also—aye, in my arrogant youth I actually despised her—poor, good-natured Mrs. Rix, who only desired my happiness. If her notion of happiness were not mine, why blame her? As I afterward learned, she had had a hard enough life of her own, to make her feel now that to secure meat, drink, and clothing of the best description for the whole of one's days, was, after all, not a bad thing.

But I? Oh! I could have lived on bread and water; I could have served on my knees; I could have given up every luxury, have suffered every sorrow—provided it were myself alone that suffered—if only I might never have parted from some one—*not* Sir Thomas Appleton.

Mrs. Rix talked till she was tired, and then, quite satisfied, I suppose, that silence meant acquiescence, and no doubt a little proud of her own powers of rhetoric, she bade me a kind good-night, and went up stairs.

I crouched once more on the hearth-rug, without even the little dog, feeling the loneliest creature alive. Not crying—I was past that—but trying to harden myself into beginning to endure. "*Vincit qui patitur*," my mother's favorite motto, to me had as yet no meaning. I had had such a happy life, with almost nothing to endure. Now I must begin—I must take up my burden and bear it, whatever it might be. And I must bear it alone. No more—ah! never any more—could I run to my mother, and lay my grief in her arms, and feel that her kiss took away almost every sting of pain. At least, so I thought then.

I tried to shut my eyes on the far future, and think only of to-morrow. Then I must inevitably speak to my grandfather, and ask him to give Sir Thomas a distinct

"I crouched once more on the hearth-rug."

No. If further information were required, I must say simply that I did not love him, and therefore could not marry him; and keep to that. Nobody could force out of me any thing more; and all reasonings and persuasions I must meet with that stony silence, easy enough toward ordinary persons, whom I cared as little for as for Mrs. Rix. But with my mother?—I felt a frantic desire, now, that every thing should be over and done before my mother came. Then she and I would return to the village together, and go back to our old life—with a difference—oh, what a difference!

It was not wholly pain. I deny that. Miserable and perplexed as I was, I felt at intervals content, glad—nay, proud. I had found out the great secret of life; I was a child no more, but a woman, with a woman's heart. When I thought of it, I hid my face, a burning face, though I was quite alone, yet I had no sense of shame. To be ashamed, indeed, because I had seen the best, the highest, and loved it! Mrs. Rix had said, *apropos* of my "shyness," that of course no girl ought to care for any man until he asked her. But I thought the angels, looking down into my poor heart, might look with other eyes than did Mrs. Rix.

So I was not ashamed. Not even when the door suddenly opened, and Cousin Conrad himself came in. I sprang up, and made believe I had been warming myself at the fire—that was all.

"I beg your pardon, Elma, but your grandfather sent me here to see if you had gone to bed."

"I was just going. Does he want me?"

"No."

Conrad was so quiet that I perforce grew quiet too, even when he came and sat down by me on the sofa.

"Have you a few minutes to spare? Because the General asked me to speak to you about a matter which you must surely guess. Shall I say my few words now, or put them off till morning?"

"Say them now."

For I felt that whatever was to happen had best happen at once, and then be over and done.

Our conversation did not last very long, but I remember it, almost word for word, even to this day. Throughout, he was his own natural self—calm, gentle, kind. I could see he had never the slightest idea he was wounding me, stabbing me deep down to the heart with such a tender hand.

"I suppose you know," he said, "what I am desired to speak to you about?"

"I think I do."

"And I hope you know also that I should not take the liberty—brotherly liberty though it be, for I feel to you like an elder brother—if the General had not expressly desired it, and if I were not afraid of any excitement bringing on a return of his illness. You would be very sorry for that."

"Yes." Yes and No were all the words I found myself capable of answering.

"Your grandfather is, as you perceive, very proud of you—fond of you, too. In his sort of way, he has set his heart upon your making what he calls a good marriage. Now, Sir Thomas Appleton—"

I turned and looked him full in the face. I wished to find out how far he spoke from his heart, and how far in accordance with his duty and my grandfather's desire.

"Sir Thomas Appleton is not a brilliantly clever man, nor, in all things, exactly the man I should have expected would please you; but he would please almost any girl, and he is thoroughly good, upright, and gentlemanly. In worldly advantages this is, as your grandfather and Mrs. Rix say" (he slightly smiled), "a very 'good' marriage indeed. Nor, I think, would your mother disapprove of it, nor need you do so, for her sake. You will be married sometime, I suppose; she knows that. This marriage would secure to her a home for life, in the house of a son-in-law who I doubt not would be as good a son to her as he always was to his own mother. Elma, are you listening?"

Of course I was! I heard every word—took in with a cruel certainty that if I said "Yes," it would make every body happy, most likely Cousin Conrad too.

"You wish me, then — you all wish me — to marry Sir Thomas Appleton, whether I care for him or not?"

He noticed the excessive bitterness of my tone. "No, you mistake. In fact, I must be in some mistake too. I thought, from what they said, that there was not the slightest doubt you cared for him. At least that his love was not unacceptable to you."

"Love!" I said fiercely. "He has danced with me half-a-dozen times at a ball, and talked with me at two or three evening parties. How can he love me? What does he know of me? As much as I of him—which is nothing, absolutely nothing. How dare he say he loves me?"

I stood with my heart throbbing and my eyes burning. I wished to do something—to hurt something or somebody, I was so hurt and sore myself. And then I fell a-crying; not violently, but the great tears would roll down. I was terribly ashamed of myself. When I looked up again, I am sure there must have been something in my eyes—he once told me I had deer's eyes—not unlike a deer when the hunter stands over her with his knife at her throat.

"Cousin Conrad, why do you persuade me to marry your friend, when I don't love him, when I don't want to marry him or any body, but only to go home to my mother? Oh, why can't you leave us at peace together? We were so happy, my mother and I?"

I broke into one single sob. At the moment my only thought was to hide myself from him and all the world in my mother's arms.

Cousin Conrad looked much troubled. "There has been some great blunder," he said, "and the General must have been utterly misled. I am glad he sent me to speak to you instead of speaking himself; for when he finds out the truth, he will be, I fear, exceedingly—disappointed. And for poor Sir Thomas, was it such a very unnatural and wicked thing to love you?" And he went on speaking with great kindliness, touching kindliness, of the many good qualities of the man who wanted to marry me—me, simple Elma Picardy, without fortune or accomplishments, or any thing to recommend me, except perhaps my poor pretty face. A generous love, at any rate, and I could perceive he thought it so.

It was very hard to bear. Even now, at this distance of time, I repeat that it was very hard to bear. For a moment, in an impulse of sharp pain, I felt inclined to do as many a girl has done under like circumstances—to throw myself, just as I was, into the refuge of a good man's love, where I should suffer no more, be blamed no more; where all my secret would be covered over, and nobody would ever know. And then I looked at the noble, good face that from my first glance at it had seemed distinct from every face I ever beheld, except my mother's.

No, I could not do it. Not while he stood there, alone in the world, with no tie that made it wrong for me to think of him as I did. I *must* think of him. I *must* love him. Though it killed me, I must love him, and never dream of marrying any body else.

So I said, quite quietly, that I should be very much obliged to him if he would take the trouble of telling my grandfather the real state of the case, as I feared this morning I did not make him understand. In truth I was so terribly frightened.

"Poor child! But you are not afraid of me? You know I would never urge you to do any thing that made you unhappy? My dear Elma, of course you shall go back to your mother. Believe me, very few of us are worth giving up a mother for."

He patted my hand. Oh, why could I not snatch it away? What a horrible hypocrite I did feel!

"And now let us see what can be done, for it is rather difficult. I have to go away early to-morrow morning, and shall probably be absent the whole week. In the mean time it will never do for you and your grandfather to talk this over together; he will get irritated with you."

"Oh let me go home to my mother!"

"She expressly said you were on no account to go, but to wait till she came or sent for you."

This was odd, but I did not take it much into account then. I was too perplexed and miserable.

"The only way that I can see is to tell your grandfather that some difficulties have arisen, and that I have gone to Sir Thomas to beg him not to urge his suit until Mrs. Picardy arrives. The General will accept that explanation, and think no more about it till the week is ended. You know, Elma, your grandfather has one very strong peculiarity: he does not like being 'bothered.'"

And Cousin Conrad smiled, just to win back my faint smile, I thought, and make me feel that life was not the dreadful tragedy which no doubt my looks implied that I found it.

"This is your first pain, my child, but it will soon pass over. I wish I could say the same for poor Appleton."

I hung my head. "Have I been to blame? Have I said or done any thing amiss? No, I am sure I have not. When one does not feel love, one can not show it."

"Some girls can, but not you. No, it is simply a misfortune, and not your fault at all. I will go and tell him the truth. He will get over it."

"I hope so." And I felt as if a load were taken off my heart, all the oppressive love (which I did not very much believe in), all the horses and carriages, houses, servants, and diamonds. I was again Elma Picardy, with her own free heart in her bosom, her heart which nobody wanted—at least nobody that could have it—and her life before her, straight and clear. Sad it might be, a little dreary perhaps sometimes, but it was quite clear.

So we sat together, Cousin Conrad and I, having arranged this unpleasant business — sat in our old way over the fire, talking a little before we bade good-night.

"Isn't it strange," said he, "that I should always be mixed up with other people's love affairs—I who have long given up every thing of the kind for myself? One would think I was a woman, and not a man, by the way people confide in me sometimes."

I thought it was because of the curious mixture of the woman in him, as there is in all good men, the very manliest of them; but I only said it was "because he was so kind."

"It would be hard not to be kind, seeing how sad the world is, and how much every body has to suffer. You, too, Elma—I don't expect you will find life a bed of roses. But I hope it will be a reasonably happy life, and not a lonely one like mine."

He paused a little, looking steadily into the fire, and folding his hands one upon the other, after his habit.

"Not that I complain—all that is, is best. And no doubt I could change my life if I chose, since, without vanity, women are so good that I could probably get some kind soul to take me if I wished it. But I do not wish it. My health is so uncertain that I have no right to ask any young woman to marry me, and I am afraid

I should not like an old one. So I'll go on as I do, and perhaps finally die in the arms of a Sister of Charity."

He was not looking at me, or thinking of me; probably he was thinking of her who died in his arms, and whom he would meet again one day. Suddenly he turned round and seized both my hands, with his whole aspect changed, the grave, composed, middle-aged face looking almost young, the sallow cheeks glowing, the lips quivering.

"I hope you will have a happy life. I hope you will find some good man whom you love, who will love you and take care of you—'wear you in his bosom,' as the song says, 'lest his jewel he should tine.' For underneath that beauty which you despise so, Elma, is a rich jewel—your heart; and I am sure your mother knows it. If you see her before I return, tell her I said so. And good-night, my dear child."

He wrung my hands and quitted the room.

Miserable girl that I was!—until he named her, I had wholly forgotten my mother!

CHAPTER XI.

I HAD wished, in telling my story, to speak as little as possible of myself and my feelings, but it is difficult to avoid it, so vividly do I recall the emotions of that time.

If I were asked at what period of a woman's life she is capable of the intensest love, the sharpest grief, I should say it was in her teens, when she is supposed too young to understand either, and late in life, when people think she ought to have done with both. Chiefly because, when young, we can scarcely take in the future; when old, we know that for us the future exists no more. Therefore I am much more sorry for girls and middle-aged women, when "in love," as the phrase is, than I am for those in the prime of life, to whom that very fact brings strength and compensation.

Falling asleep that night, or rather next morning, for it was daylight before I lost consciousness of myself and what had happened to me within those thirty-six hours—I was a changed creature. Not a miserable creature at all, not in the least broken-hearted, only changed.

I knew now that for me woman's natural lot, to which my mother looked innocently forward, was not to be. I should never marry, never give her the grandchildren that she used to laugh about, or the son-in-law that was to be the staff of her old age. For me, and for her through me, these felicities were quite at an end. Yet I did not grieve. I felt rather a kind of solemn contentment, a peaceful acceptance of every thing; my lot, if not happy in the ordinary sense, would be very blessed, for I should never lose him—he would never marry; nobody was likely ever to be a nearer friend to him than I. And I might, in my own humble way, come very near to him. The chances of life were so many, that to a faithful heart, continually on the watch to do him good or to be of use to him, innumerable opportunities might arise. Nay, even if I were quite passive, never able to do any thing for him, I might still watch him from a distance, glory in his goodness, sympathize in his cares, and feel that I belonged to him in some far-off way that nobody knew of, to the end of my days.

That sad word he had let fall about the end of *his* days being so uncertain did not affect me much. At my age, to one who has never come near it, death seems merely a phantom, often more beautiful than sad—a shadow that may fall upon others, but does not touch ourselves. To me, with my heart full of new-born love, death seemed a thing unnatural and impossible. I never remember thinking of him and it together, no more than if he had been immortal, as to me he truly was.

Thus, after our conversation that night, I was quite happy—happier than I had ever been in my life before. My feeling was, in a dim sort of way, almost that of a person betrothed—betrothed to some one who had gone to a far country, or whom she could not possibly marry; yet having a sense of settled peace, such as girls never have whose hearts are empty and their destinies uncertain. Mine was, I believed, fixed forever; I had no need to trouble about it any more.

And though I was so young, not yet eighteen, what did it matter? My grandmother was married at eighteen. So in a sense was I. I took one of my mother's rings (the very few she possessed she had given me when I left her) and placed it on the third finger; now nobody need attempt to marry me any more.

Three days passed by—three perfectly quiet days. My

grandfather was not well, and kept his rooms. Mrs. Rix never said a word to me about Sir Thomas Appleton, or any thing. She was a little distant and cold, as if I had somehow done a foolish or naughty thing, and thereby made myself of much less value than I was a few days before; but that was all the difference I found in her. It was Cousin Conrad, I knew, who had smoothed matters down for me, even when absent, though how he managed it I never knew.

The letter I had expected from my mother did not come, nor she herself either. It surprises me now to remember how calmly I took this, and how easily I satisfied myself that, being quite unaware of the reason she had been sent for, she was waiting patiently till my grandfather should send for her again. Also, though I watched the post daily, with an anxiety that I tried hard to conceal, it was not entirely for my mother's letters.

Cousin Conrad had said that he should probably send me a line from London. A letter from him—a bit of his own handwriting, and for me! No wonder I waited for it, and rejoiced in it when it came, with a joy the reflected shadow of which lingers even now.

The merest line it was:

"DEAR COUSIN ELMA,—Tell your mother I have procured the books she wanted, and hope to bring them to her next week, if she is not with you, as I trust she is. No more, for I am very busy, but always

"Your affectionate friend,

"CONRAD PICARDY."

My "affectionate friend!" It was enough, enough to make my life happy until the end. So I believed then; perhaps I do still. The heart of life is the love that is in it, and the worthiness of the person loved.

I wrote to my mother, giving Cousin Conrad's message, and scolding her gayly for not having come or written. I said if she did not appear to-morrow, I should most certainly come and see her. Only come and see her; I did not suggest coming home for good. I reasoned with myself it would be so very much better for her to come here.

All my happy dreams revived, all my plans concerning her and him, and how they would care for one another, and I for them both. As to myself, I must try to make myself worth caring for; try to cultivate my mind, and even to make the most of my outside beauty, which he had told me I "despised." He did not; he liked beautiful people, and owned it. Was not Agnes beautiful, and, as Mrs. Rix once said, just a little like me?

Once or twice, by ingeniously guiding the conversation, I had got Mrs. Rix to talk of Agnes; for I loved her almost as if she had been alive—loved them both together, for, in a human sense, both were equally distant from me—distant, yet so near. The thought of him was now never absent from me for a single minute, not displacing other thoughts, but accompanying them like an under-current of singing birds or murmuring streams; or, rather, it was most like what I have heard nursing mothers say when they went to sleep with a baby in their arms: they were never afraid either of harming or forgetting it, because, waking or sleeping, they were always conscious it was there. So was I. My last sigh of prayer at night was for him; my first feeling in the morning was how bright and happy the world seemed, since he was in it! A world without him, a day in which I could not wake up to the thought of him, appeared now incredible and impossible.

I know there are those who will smile, and call such a love, such a worship rather, equally incredible and impossible. I do not argue the point. That it was a truth my life has proved.

The third day after that day—so full of startling pain, yet ending in solemn content—I was sitting peacefully sewing in my bedroom, whither, on any excuse, I was glad to creep. To be alone was the greatest bliss I knew. My watch, ticking on the table beside me, was the only sound that broke the quietness. I looked tenderly at its pretty white face, and thought of Cousin Conrad's mother, and what a happy woman she must have been, and how I would have loved her had I known her.

Then, seeing it was near post-time, I listened, but not anxiously. It was unlikely he would write again before he came back on the following Wednesday, three days hence. Then he would be sure to come. One of his characteristics was exceeding punctuality and dependableness. If he had promised to do a certain thing at a certain time, you might rely upon him that no whim, no fancy, no variable change of plan, nothing, in short, but inevitable necessity, would prevent his doing it. Down to the smallest trifles, he was the most conscientious person I ever knew. Once when I told him so he laughed, and said, "Life was so full of work that if one did not take some trouble to make it all fit in together, like the wheels of a watch, the whole machinery soon went wrong."

But I am wandering from my actual story—wandering away to linger over this picture of a perfect life. For his was an almost perfect life. Some women's destiny is to love down, excusingly, pityingly. Thank God! mine was to love up.

I sat thinking of him, and wondering how he had settled that troublesome business in London which he had told me of—other people's business, of course—sat as happy as could be, as unconscious of the footstep of coming sorrow as (mercifully, I often think) we generally are until it knocks at our very door. Thus, for the second time, under Mrs. Rix's fingers it knocked at mine.

"Come down at once to the General; he has got a letter."

"From my mother?" But though I said "my mother," I thought not of her alone, and if I turned sick with dread, my fear was not wholly on her account.

"No, my poor dear girl, not exactly your mother. The doctor—"

"Oh, she is ill! she is ill!" And pushing Mrs. Rix aside, I ran down stairs like lightning and burst into my grandfather's room. He gave me the letter at once.

My darling mother! Her week of silence, her not coming to Bath, as well as her anxiety to prevent my coming home, were now fully accounted for. Small-pox had been very much about in the village, and at last she had caught it—not dangerously, the doctor said hers was a mild case; still she had been very ill, and it would be some time yet before she was able to write. He wrote, by her desire, to my grandfather, explaining all, and entreating that I should be kept from coming to her. She had all the care she needed—himself, Mrs. Golding, and a hospital nurse—and nothing must be risked for her child. On no account was I to come near her.

"Cruel! cruel!" sobbed I, till I met my grandfather's look of amazement. "No, it is not cruel; it is just like herself—just what she always told me she would do in such a case. She used to say that she should have lived alone but for me, and she could die alone, even without one sight of me, rather than harm me. Oh, mother! mother!"

I think my grandfather was touched, and that if he bore any grudge against me in the matter of Sir Thomas he forgot it now. His tone and manner were extremely kind.

"Comfort yourself, my dear; you see all has gone well so far; Mrs. Picardy is apparently out of danger, and no doubt will soon be convalescent. She was quite right to act as she did; I respect her for it, and shall tell the doctor so, desiring him to pay her all attention, and send news of her every day."

"News every day!" For, in spite of all my mother's prohibitions, I had no thought but how fast I could get ready, and, imploring for once to have the carriage, go home immediately.

"Yes, every day, or every other day, as he says it is a mild case," continued my grandfather, looking a little wearied of my tears; "and if Mrs. Rix could suggest any thing to send her—wine or jelly, perhaps—provided we run no risk of infection. Pardon me, but I have a great horror of small-pox. In my young days it was an actual scourge. Two young ladies I knew had their prospects blighted for life by it; but your excellent mother is neither very young nor—"

"She is beautiful—beautiful to me!" cried I, indignantly. "She is every thing that is sweet and precious to me. Oh, if she had only told me she was ill—if I could have gone to her days ago!"

"You do not mean to say you are going now?"

Had I meant it? I can not tell. I was silent.

"Such a step," my grandfather continued, "would be most imprudent. She herself forbids it, and I respect her for doing so. You could not benefit her, and you might destroy your prospects for life."

Destroy my prospects for life! Probably because he, too, considered that my face was my fortune, and the small-pox might spoil me and prevent my being married by some other Sir Thomas Appleton! That thought settled my mind at once.

I said, with a quietness that surprised myself, considering the storm of grief and rage within me, "I do not care for my prospects. Since it is for my sake only that my mother forbids my going to her, I mean to disobey her and go."

Then, for the first time, I saw what my grandfather could be when he was contradicted. Peace be to him! I had rather not remember any thing he said, nor recall the expression of his noble and handsome old face, as I saw it just then. He must, as I found out afterward, have built many hopes and plans upon poor me, the last of his direct line, and it was hard to have them disappointed.

"You will understand one thing," said he at last, his

wrath turning from a red into a white heat, equally powerful and more dangerous, "when you quit this house against my will, you quit it forever. All that I mean to give you I shall leave to your Cousin Conrad. You hear me?"

"Oh yes!" And I was so glad!—glad that he should have all, and I nothing; that in any way my loss should be his gain. But the next minute I heard something more.

"Now, Elma, I will detain you no longer. If you have your vexations, I have mine. Only this morning Conrad writes to tell me he is going back to India immediately."

I have heard people, who have suffered sudden anguishes, say that it is like a gun-shot wound, which at first does not hurt at all. The struck man actually stands upright a minute, sometimes with a smile on his face, before he drops. So it was with me.

Had my grandfather seen me, I believe there would have been nothing to see; but he put his hand over his face, and spoke querulously rather than angrily.

"So make up your mind—if any woman ever could make up her mind. Stay, and I will send daily for news of your mother. Go, and though it is a fool's errand, my carriage shall take you there in safety. But, remember, you do not return. Adieu now. In an hour let me have your decision."

He rose, and bowed me out of his study with cold politeness—me, a poor girl whose mother was dying!

But I did not believe that; indeed, I must have accepted blindly the doctor's statement that it was a mild case, and the worst over, and I must have deluded my conscience in the most extraordinary way as to the sin of disobeying my grandfather, as well as my mother. Still, looking back, I can pity myself. It was a hard strait for a poor girl to be in, even without that other thing, which nobody knew of.

But *I* knew it. I—the inner me—was perfectly well aware that my worst struggle was with another pang, and that the difficulty of choice sprang from quite another motive than the dread of vexing my grandfather, or even of saving myself—my young life and my pretty face—which had, nevertheless, grown strangely dear to me of late.

If I went back to my mother, and Cousin Conrad went to India in a month, I should not see him again—perhaps never in this world. For even if he wished to come to bid me good-by, my grandfather would prevent it. I, too, perhaps. Of course I should treat him exactly as my mother had treated me, and shut the door of our infected house upon him, even though it broke my heart. Therefore, if I went away to-day, I should never look upon his face, never hear the sound of his voice—never any more!

Oh, my God! my God!

I believe I did instinctively cry out that upon him, conscious for the first time in my brief life that he has it in his power to take away the desire of our eyes at a stroke. My mother—Cousin Conrad—I might lose them both. Nay, by holding to one I should infallibly lose the other. What must I do?

I did that which we are all so prone to do—I temporized. I said to myself that for a girl like me to fly in the face of her grandfather and her mother was very wrong; that if I literally obeyed them, whatever followed, they could not blame me. At any rate, I would obey till Wednesday, when I should see Cousin Conrad, and could ask him, whose judgment of right and wrong was so clear and firm, what I ought to do.

Oh, sad sophistry! trying with vain arguments to reason myself into doing what I wanted to do, following the compulsion of an emotion so overwhelming, an agony so sharp and new, that I could not comprehend it or myself. Even with my mother in my heart all the time—wretched about her, longing to go and take care of her—I felt that at all risks, at all costs, I must stay and look on that other face—the only face that ever came between me and hers—just once more.

Within an hour I knocked at my grandfather's door, and told him I would stay, at any rate, for one day more—I dared not say two days, lest he might guess why. But no, he seemed almost to have forgotten what I came about till I reminded him.

"Certainly, certainly; we will send a messenger off at once to inquire, and I hope your mother will be quite well soon; she is sure to agree with me that you have acted wisely. And for myself, I am much gratified by your remaining with me. When Conrad is gone, I shall have only you left to be a comfort to my old age."

He patted my hand almost with tenderness. Oh, what a hypocrite I felt!

Most of those two days I spent in his study. He seemed to like to have me, and I liked to be there. It was easier to busy myself in doing things for him than to sit with my hands before me, thinking or listening to Mrs. Rix's terrible flow of talk. Poor woman, she was so torturingly kind to me—helped me pack up the basket of good things, giving strict injunctions that it should be dropped outside the door, and that the messenger should on no account go in. She hovered over me while I wrote the letter that was to accompany it, sympathizing with my torrents of tears, yet telling me no end of stories about families she knew, who had been swept off wholesale by the small-pox, or made hideous for life.

"If it were any thing but small-pox, my dear, I should say, go at once. A mother is a mother, you know. When mine was in her last illness, I sat up with her night after night for three weeks. The last forty-eight hours I never left her for an instant—not till the breath was out of her body. I closed her eyes my own self, my dear, and thankful, too, for she had suffered very much."

"Oh, be quiet—be quiet!" I almost screamed; and then the good woman kissed me, with her tears running down, and was silent—for about three minutes.

Her next attempt to change the subject was concerning "poor Major Picardy" and his sudden return to India, wondering why he went, when he could so easily have retired on half-pay or sold out; in the course of nature it could not be very long before he came in for the Picardy estate. "The property he must have; though, as I told you, your grandfather can leave the ready money to any body else—you, perhaps, since he is much vexed at the Major's departure. Besides, India doubles the risk of his health, and if he die, where is the estate to go to?—not that he is likely ever to be an old man. Still, he might pull on with care, poor fellow! for a good many years. But I suppose he thinks it does not much matter whether his life is long or short, seeing he has neither wife nor child. He said as much to me the other day."

I did not believe that—it was contrary to his reticent character; but I believed a great deal. And I listened—listened as a St. Sebastian must have listened to the whiz of each arrow that struck him—until I felt something like the picture of that poor young saint in the

National Gallery, which my mother and I used to stop and look at. She was rather fond of pictures in the old days.

Ah, those days! Six months ago I would no more have thought of keeping away from her when she was ill, had she commanded it ever so, than of not pulling her out of a river for fear of wetting my hand! Sometimes, strangely as I was deceiving myself about the duty of obedience, and so on, there flashed across me a vivid sense of what a cowardly, selfish wretch I was, even though my motive was no foolish fear for my pretty face, or even my poor young life, the whole preciousness of which hung on other lives, which might or might not last.

Once, on the Tuesday evening, when I was taking a walk with Mrs. Rix, who had benignly given up a card-party; when the birds were singing their last sleepy song, the sky was so clear and the earth so sweet, I had such a vision of my mother lying sick in her bed, all alone, perhaps neglected—at any rate without me beside her, me, her own daughter, who knew all her little ways, and could nurse her as no one else could—that a great horror seized me. Had it not been night, I believe I should have started off that minute and gone to her, even had I walked the whole way.

With difficulty Mrs. Rix got me to go in and go to bed—Mrs. Rix, the poor, dear woman whose arguments I despised; yet I yielded, saying to myself, "It is only twelve hours to wait."

Wait for what? The message from my mother or the one more look at Cousin Conrad's face, the one last clasp of his hand, and then it would all be shut up in my heart forever—the love he did not care for, the grief he could not see. I should just bid him good-by, an ordinary good-by, and go back to my mother, to begin again the old life—with a difference. But the difference only concerned myself. Nobody else should be troubled by it. If I were careful, even she should not find it out.

So, with a kind of stolid patience and acceptance of whatever might happen, without struggling against it any more, I laid me down to sleep that Tuesday night, and woke up on Wednesday morning—a very bright, sunshiny morning, I remember, it was—much as those wake up who, in an hour or two, are to be led outside their prison walls to feel the sunshine, to see the blue sky, just for a few minutes, and then, in their full young strength, with every capacity of enjoyment, "aimer et d'être aimé" (as wrote a young Frenchman, Roussel, who thus perished, in the terrible later revolution that I have lived to see), be placed blindfold against a wall and—shot.

CHAPTER XII.

I SPENT most of the Wednesday morning in my grandfather's study, reading aloud his daily newspapers, writing some letters, and doing other little things for him which Cousin Conrad was used to do.

"But you may as well begin to learn to help me; there will be nobody else to do it when he is gone," said the old man sadly.

One quality, which my mother used to say was the balance-weight that guided all others, she often thought me sorely deficient in—self-control. I think I began to learn it during these last days, and especially that Wednesday morning.

Several times my grandfather praised me quite affectionately for my "quietness." "One might suppose you were two or three and twenty, my dear, instead of not yet eighteen."

Not yet eighteen! What a long, dreary expanse of life seemed before me, if I took after him and the family (the Picardys, save during this last generation, have been a long-lived race), and attained to the mysterious threescore years and ten! Yet, in a sort of way, he was happy still.

But I—I shivered at the prospect, and wondered how I should ever bear it all.

Now I wonder no more. I think it will be so. Like him, I shall probably live to extreme old age; the last leaf on the tree: very lonely, but not forlorn. Yet I accept the fact, and do not complain. God never leaves any life without sunshine while it can find its sunshine in his smile.

Cousin Conrad had not said what time he should arrive, and I thought every ring at the hall-bell was his. When at last he came, it was without any warning. He just walked in as if he had left us yesterday, and all things were the same as yesterday.

"General! Cousin Elma! How very cosy you look, sitting together!" And he held out a hand to each of us.

Then he sat down, and he and my grandfather fell into talk at once about his going to India.

I would have slipped away, but nobody told me to go away, or seemed to make any more account of me than if I were a chair or a table. So I took up a book and stayed. It would have been dreadful to have to go. Even a few additional minutes in his presence was something. Of my own affairs nobody said a word, and for the moment all remembrance of them passed from me. I only sat in my corner and gazed and gazed.

He looked ill, and perhaps a shade graver than usual; but the sweet expression of the mouth was unchanged, and so was the wonderful look in the eyes, calm, far-away, heavenly, such as I have never seen in any human eyes but his.

At that moment, aye, and many a time, I thought—if I could just have died for him, without his knowing it! died and left him happy for the rest of his life; yes, even though it had been with some other woman—how content I should have been!

My grandfather and he began talking earnestly. To all the General's arguments he answered very little.

"No, I have no particular reason for going—at least, none of any consequence to any body but myself. As you say, perhaps I am weary of idleness, and there lies work which I can do, and come back again in a few years."

"To find me in my grave."

"Not you; you will be a hale octogenarian, and that young lady," turning to look at me, "will be a blooming young matron. By-the-bye, Cousin Elma, did you give my message to your mother? I hope she is quite well."

I could bear no more. I burst into violent sobs. He came over to me at once.

"What is the matter? What has happened?" Then in a whisper, "Surely, my little jest did not offend you?"

Evidently, he knew nothing; but my grandfather soon told him all.

"What! her mother ill, and Elma still here?"

This was all he said. Not in any reproach or blame, but in a kind of sad surprise. At once, as by a flash of lightning, I saw the right and the wrong of things; how I had acted, and what he must have thought of me for so acting.

"She is here, because I would not allow her to go," said my grandfather, hastily and half apologetically, as if he, too, had read Cousin Conrad's look. "Mrs. Picardy herself, with extreme good sense, forbade her coming. Think what a risk the girl would run. As a man of the world, Conrad, you must be aware that with her beauty—"

"Yes, I am aware of every thing; but still I say she should have gone."

It was spoken very gently, so gently that even my grandfather could not take offense. For me, all I did was frantically to implore Cousin Conrad to help me to persuade my grandfather to let me go. I would run any risks. I did not care what happened to myself at all.

"I know that, poor child. Hush! and I will try to arrange it for you."

He put me into an arm-chair, very tenderly, and stood by me, holding my hand, as a sort of protection, if such were needed. But it was not. Either my grandfather had seen his mistake, or did not care very much about

"Was it fancy, or did I feel the kind hand closed tighter over mine?"

the matter either way, so that he was not "bothered;" or else—let me give the highest and best motive to him, as we always should to every body—before many more words had been said, he felt by instinct that Cousin Conrad was right.

"Elma has shown her good feeling and obedience to me by not going at first," said he with dignity. "Now, if you think it advisable, and if, as I suppose, the risk is nearly over—"

"No, it is not over. Do not let us deceive ourselves." Was it fancy, or did I feel the kind hand closed tighter over mine? "For all that, she ought to go."

At that moment Mrs. Rix came in, looking very much troubled. She had met the messenger returning with the news that "Mrs. Picardy was not quite so well to-day."

"Order the carriage at once," said my grandfather, abruptly.

Then there was a confused hurrying of me out of the room, packing up of my things, talking, talking—poor, kind Mrs. Rix could do nothing without talking!—but, in spite of all the haste, at the end of an hour I was still standing in my bedroom, watching stonily every body doing every thing for me. Oh, they were so kind, so terribly kind, as people constantly are to those unto whom they think something is going to happen; and they gave me endless advice about nursing my mother and saving myself—I who knew nothing at all about small-pox or any kind of illness, who had never in my life been laid on a sick-bed or stood beside one. They were sorry for me, I think; for I remember even the little kitchen-maid coming up and pressing a little bag of camphor into my hand.

"Take care of yourself, miss; oh, do take care of your pretty face," said she; but I paid no attention to her or to any body.

The one person who did not come near me was Cousin Conrad. I thought I should have had to go without bidding him good-by, when I saw him standing at the drawing-room door.

"Here, Mrs. Rix, I want to consult you."

And then he explained that he had fetched a doctor, whose new theory it was that second vaccination was a complete preservative against small-pox — that every thing was ready to do it if I would consent.

"You will not refuse? You think only of your mother. But I—we—must think also of you."

"Thank you," I said; "you are very kind." He could not help being kind to any creature in trouble.

Without more ado I bared my arm. I remember I wore what in those days was called a tippet and sleeves, so it was easy to get at it; but when the doctor took out his case of instruments I began to tremble a little.

"Will it hurt much?—Not that I mind." In truth, I

should not have minded being killed, with his hand to hold by, and his pitying eyes looking on.

"Do not be frightened. It hurts no more than the prick of a pin," said Cousin Conrad, cheerfully; "only it leaves a rather ugly mark. Stop a minute, Doctor. Mrs. Rix, push the sleeve a little farther up. Do not let us spoil her pretty arm."

The doctor called for somebody to hold it.

"I will," he said, seeing Mrs. Rix looked frightened. She said she could not bear the sight of the smallest "surgical operation." "Not that this is one. But if it were," added he, with a look I have never forgotten, "I think I should prefer nobody to hurt you but me."

There was a silent minute, and then the doctor paused.

"I forgot to ask if this young lady is likely to be in the way of small-pox just at present, because, if so, vaccination might double the risk instead of lessening it. She ought to keep from every chance of infection for ten or twelve days."

I said, with strange quietness, "It is of no consequence—I must go. My mother may be dead in ten or twelve days."

Cousin Conrad stopped the surgeon's hand. "If it be so, what are we doing? In truth I hardly know what I am doing. Let me think a moment."

I saw him put his hand to his head. Then he and the

doctor retired together, and talked apart. I sat still a minute or two, and followed them.

"I can not wait—I must go."

"You shall go, poor child," said Cousin Conrad. He was very white—long afterward I remembered this too —but he spoke quietly, soothingly, as to a child. "Listen; this is the difficult question. If you are vaccinated, and go at once to your mother, you have no chance of escaping the disease; if you are not vaccinated afresh, there is just a chance that the old protection may remain. He does not say you will escape, but you may. Will you try it? If you must go, you ought to go at once. Shall you go?"

"Of course I shall."

He drew a deep breath. "I thought she would. Doctor, you see."

"She runs a great risk," said the old man, looking at me compassionately.

"I know that—nobody better than I. Still she must go. Come, Elma, and bid your grandfather good-by."

He drew my arm through his, and we went down stairs together, Mrs. Rix following us. She was crying a little—kind, soft-hearted woman!—but I could not cry at all.

My grandfather, too, was very kind. "A sad departure, Elma. We shall all miss you very much, shall we

"He drew my arm through his."

not, Conrad? Such a bit of young bright life among us old folks!"

"Yes," said he.

"Good-by, my dear, and God bless you. Kiss me."

I did so, clinging to him as I had never clung to any body except my mother. My heart was breaking. All my cry now was to go to my mother. Indeed, the strain was becoming so dreadful, minute by minute, that I was longing to be away.

"Is any body going in the carriage with you?" said my grandfather.

Eagerly I answered that I wanted nobody, I had rather be alone; that I wished no one to come near our house, or to run the slightest danger of infection. And then they praised me, my grandfather and Mrs. Rix, for my good sense and right feeling. One person only said nothing at all!

Not till the very last moment, when I was in the carriage and he standing by it—standing bare-headed in the sunshine, looking so old, so worn. And oh, what a bright day it was! How happy all the world seemed, except me.

"If I do not come with you, it is not from fear of infection. You never thought it was?"

"No."

"That is right. And now think solely of nursing your mother and taking care of yourself. Take all the care you can. You promise?"

"Yes."

"Then good-by, and God bless you, my dearest child."

He said that—those very words. Confused as I was, I was sure of this.

A minute more, and I was gone. Gone away from him, from the sound of his voice and the sight of his face; gone away into darkness, anxiety, and pain. How sharp a pain I did not even then sufficiently recognize.

For there was remorse mixed with it—remorse that, in my passionate exaggeration of girlhood, felt to me like "the worm that dieth not, the fire that is never quenched." From the moment that the glamour passed away, and I got into the old familiar scenes—even before I entered the village—the gnawing pain began. There was no need of Mrs. Golding's bitter welcome—"So, Miss Picardy, you're come at last, and high time too!"—no need of her sarcastic answer that my mother was "going on quite well, and perfectly well attended to," to smite me to the very heart.

"Beg your pardon, miss, but as nobody expected you, the parlor isn't ready; and of course you won't think of going up stairs."

I never answered a word, but just began to feel my way up the narrow staircase. After Royal Crescent, how narrow and dark it seemed, and how close and stuffy the whole house was! Yet here my mother had been lying, alone, sick unto death, without me; while I

—Oh me, oh me! would God ever forgive me? She would, I knew; but he? Or should I ever forgive myself?

I think the sharpest conscience-sting of all is that which nobody knows of except one's self. Now no creature said to me a word of blame. Even Mrs. Golding, after her first sharp welcome, left me alone; too busy to take the slightest notice of me or my misdeeds. She and all the house seemed absorbed in their nursing. There could be no doubt how well my mother was loved, how tenderly she had been cared for.

But I—I was made no more account of than a stock or a stone.

"You can't go in," said Mrs. Golding, catching hold of me just as I reached the familiar door. "Nobody sees her but the nurse and me. And she doesn't want you. She begged and prayed that we wouldn't tell you; and when you was obliged to be told, that we'd keep you away from her. Bless her, poor dear lady, she might have saved herself that trouble."

I groaned in the anguish of my heart.

"Hold your tongue, or she'll hear you. She can't see, but her ears are sharp enough. For all she said about your not being allowed to come, she's been listening, listening every day."

"I must go in—I will go in."

"No, you won't, Miss Picardy."

And without more argument the old woman pushed me into the little room beside my mother's, shut the door, and set her back against it.

"Here you are, and here you may stop; for you're not of the least good any where else in the house. I'm sorry the room's so small—after them at Royal Crescent—and dull, for a young lady as has been going to dancing-parties and card-parties every night; but it's all we can do for you just at present. By-and-by, when your mother gets better, if she does get better, and God only knows—"

But here even the hard old woman grew softer at the sight of my despair.

Does any body know what it is—the despair of having forsaken a mother, and such a mother as mine?

In all her life she had never forgotten me, never ceased to make me her first object, first delight; and now, in her time of need, I had forgotten her, had put her in the second place, had allowed other interests and other enjoyments to fill my heart. And when it came to the point, I had taken advantage of her generous love, seized upon every feeble excuse to stay away from her, left to strangers the duty of nursing her; aye, and they had done it, while her own daughter had contented herself with mere superficial inquiries, and never come near her bedside.

This, let people pity and excuse me as they might—

and Mrs. Golding, to soothe me, did make some kindly excuses at last—was the plain truth of the matter. However others might be deceived, I could not deceive myself. If, as they hinted, my mother were to die, I should never be happy again—never in this world.

And there I was, bound hand and foot as it were; close to her, yet unable to go near her, or do any thing for her; shut up in that tiny room, afraid to stir or speak, lest she should find out I was there, which, in her critical state, both the nurse and the doctor agreed might be most dangerous. I spoke to them both, and they spoke to me those few meaningless, encouraging words that people say in such circumstances; and then they left me, every body left me, to pass hour after hour in listening for every sound within that solemn, quiet sick-chamber.

All the day, and half of the night, I sat there, perfectly passive, resisting nothing, except Mrs. Golding's efforts to get me to bed. "What was the use of my sitting up? I was no good to nobody."

Ah! that was the misery of it. I *was* "no good to nobody!" And with my deep despair there mingled a mad jealousy of all those who were any good, who were doing every thing they could think of for my darling mother, while I sat there like a stone.

Oh, it served me right—quite right. Every thing was a just punishment, for—what?

I did not even ask myself what. I gave no name to the thing—the joy or the pain—which had been at the bottom of all. From the moment I had crossed this threshold, my whole life at Bath seemed to pass away—like a dream when one awakes—as completely as if it had never been.

CHAPTER XIII.

"SLEEPING for sorrow." Some people know what that is, especially when they are young; they know also how terrible is the waking.

About midnight I had thrown myself on the bed in my clothes. Just before dawn, a twittering swallow outside awoke me, shivering with cold, wondering where I was, and why I was still dressed. Then the whole truth poured upon me like a flood.

After a while I gathered strength and confidence enough to get up and listen. All was quiet in the next room, dead quiet. Even the faint, slow stirring of the fire, the last sound I had caught before falling asleep, had ceased. Who was there? What was happening?

I opened my door noiselessly—the other door stood ajar, so that I could look in. Every thing was half-dark; the fire had dropped into red embers; the nurse sat beside it, asleep in her chair. The bed I could not see, but I heard from it faint breathing, and now and then a slight moan.

Oh, my mother! my mother!

She was saying her prayers—all alone, in the middle of the night, with not a creature to love her or comfort her; sick—dying, perhaps—dying without one sight of me. She was saying to herself the words which, she once told me, had been her consolation her whole life through—"Our Father," and "Thy will be done."

My heart felt like to burst. But the self-control which she had tried vainly to teach me, until God taught me in a different way, stood me in good stead now. Hiding behind the door, I succeeded in keeping myself perfectly quiet.

By-and-by she called feebly for "some water to drink," but getting no answer, turned over again with a patient sigh.

What should I do?—wake the nurse, or go to my mother myself—I who had been so cruelly shut out from her? But what if, as they said, I did her harm? I had had no experience whatever of sickness or sick-nursing. Suppose at the mere sight of me she should get startled, excited? And then I remembered, almost with relief, that she could not see me. The small-pox had, as often happens, for the time being made her totally blind.

She called again upon the stupid, sleeping nurse—well, poor woman, she had not been to bed for eight nights!—and called in vain. Then I determined to risk it. Stepping stealthily forward, I came beside the bed, and looked at my darling mother. Oh, what a sight!

Once I heard a poor lady say, threatened with heart-complaint, "Thank God, it is a clean disease to die of!" and the horror of so many of those illnesses which we have to fight with and suffer from is that they are just the contrary—so terribly painful both to the sick and those about them. Small-pox is one of these.

My mother had it in a comparatively mild form; that is, the eruption had not extended beyond the face and head. Yet there she lay—she, once so sweet and pure that kissing her was, I sometimes said, like kissing a bunch of violets—one mass of unpleasantness, soreness, and pain.

Wearily she moved her head from side to side, evidently not knowing where to lay it for ease, talking to herself between whiles in a helpless, patient way, "Oh, the long, long night!—Oh, I wish it was morning!—Nurse, nurse! isn't there any body to give me a drink of water?"

Then I hesitated no more. Ignorant as I was, and half stupid with misery besides, I managed to lift her up in the bed, and hold the glass to her lips with a perfectly steady hand, afterward rearranging her pillows, and making her, she said, "so comfortable." This I did not once, but several times. Yet she never found me out. She said, "Thank you, nurse," and seemed a little surprised at not being answered; but that was all. Sickness was too heavy upon her to take much notice of any thing. And then the nursing she had had was mere mechanical doing of what was necessary, not caressingly, not what a daughter's would have been. Poor darling! as she lay back again in her patient darkness, not seeming even to expect any thing—not one soothing word or touch—her poor hands folded themselves in the same meek resignation.

"Pray go to your bed, nurse. I will try to go to sleep again."

I kept silence. It was for her sake, and I did it; but it was one of the hardest things I ever had to do in all my life. Until morning I sat beside my mother, she utterly unconscious of my presence, and I thinking of nothing and nobody but her.

Yes, it was so. The sight of her poor face blotted out entirely every other face—even his. This was the real life—the dream-life was gone. As I sat there, quite quiet now, not even crying silently, as at first I had done, all that I said to myself was that vow which another girl made—not to her own mother, only her mother-in-law—"God do so to me, and more also, if aught but death part thee and me."

I think I could have restrained myself, and managed so cleverly that for hours my mother might never have found me out, had not Mrs. Golding suddenly entered the room with a flash of daylight, waking up the nurse, and coming face to face with me as I sat, keeping watch in her stead.

"Bless my soul, you here? Go away directly."

I said in a whisper, but with a resolution she could not mistake, "I shall not go away. I have been here half the night. No one shall nurse my mother but me."

Sick people often take things much more quietly than we expect. All things come alike to them; they are surprised at nothing. My mother only said—

"Mrs. Golding, who is it that you want to send away? Who says she has been sitting with me half the night? Was it my child?"

"Yes, mother darling, and you'll let me stay? I'll be such a good nurse—and I'll never go to sleep at all."

She laughed—a little, low, contented laugh—and put out her hand; then suddenly seemed to recollect herself, and drew it back.

"You ought not to have come—I told you not to come."

"It is too late now, for I have been here, as I said, half the night; and didn't I make you comfortable?"

"Oh, so comfortable! Oh, how glad I am to have my child!"

This was all she said, or I. People do not talk much under such circumstances. Even Mrs. Golding forbore to blame or scold, but stood with the tea-cup in her hand until a large tear dropped into it. Then she gave it up to me, and disappeared.

The nurse followed her, a little vexed, perhaps; but they both recovered themselves in time, and allowed me to take my place beside my mother without much opposition. Truly I was, as they said, "a young, ignorant, helpless thing," but they saw I tried to do my best, and it was my right to do it.

So I did it, making a few mistakes, no doubt, out of utter inexperience; but out of carelessness, never. My whole mind was set upon one thing—how I could best take care of my mother. Of those words which, when uttered, had shot through me with such a sense of joy, "Take care of yourself," I never once thought again, or of him who had said them. For the first time in my life, I learned the utter absorption of a sick-room—how every thing seems to centre within its four narrow walls, and every thing in the world without seems to fade away and grow dim in the distance. No fear of my forgetting my mother now.

It was very painful sick-nursing, the most painful I think I ever knew, and I have known much in my lifetime. The mere physical occupation of it put out every other thought, leaving no single minute for either hopes or fears. To keep stolidly on, doing every thing that could be done, day by day, and hour by hour—that was all. As for dread of infection, or anxiety as to what would happen next, to her or to me, I do not remember even thinking of these things. Except that it was just her and me, my mother and I, as heretofore, shut up together in that one room, with the eye of God looking upon us—we uncertain what it would be his will to do; whether, in any way, either by taking her and leaving me, or healing her and smiting me—I deserved it! oh, how intensely I sometimes felt that I deserved it!—he would part mother and child.

He did it not. She slowly recovered, and by one of those mysterious chances which now and then occur with small-pox, I, though running every danger of it, never took the disease. They all watched me—I could see how they watched me, with a kind of anxious pity that I never felt for myself; but day after day went by, and still I kept perfectly well, able for all that I had to do, never once breaking down either in body or mind. My mother sometimes followed me about the room with a tender content in her eyes.

"I used to wonder what sort of woman my child would grow up—now I know."

We had "turned the tables," she and I; she was weak, I strong. Naturally, illness made her a little restless and querulous; I was always calm. In fact, as I told her laughing once, she was the baby, and I the old woman. Yes, that was the greatest change in me—I began to feel so very old.

That did not matter—heaven had preserved my mother, and me too, though I had taken my life in my hand to win or lose. It was saved. I was kept to fight on and labor on all these years, and at last, I suppose, to be laid in my coffin with the same face which, even to this day, those who love me are pleased to call beautiful.

But my mother's face was changed, though she recovered; and when she really began to mend, more rapidly than any one expected, still the disease left its mark upon her soft cheeks, her pretty neck and throat, round which, when I was quite a big girl, my sleepy hand loved to creep in babyish fashion. The expression of her dear face could not alter, but her complexion, once fresh as a child's, totally faded. When I left her, that day she stood at the door, and watched the carriage drive away, she had still looked young; when she rose up from her sick-bed, she was almost an elderly woman.

Still, this also did not matter. People do not love their mothers as knights their ladye-loves, or husbands their wives, for the sake of their youth and beauty; though I have known of chivalric devotion to a very plain woman, and tender love to a wife both feeble and old. When I got my mother once more down stairs, and had her in my arms safe and sound, warm and alive, I think no lover ever wept over his mistress more passionate, more joyful tears. Her poor, faded face counted for nothing. Only to think, as I say, that she was safe and alive—that I had fought for her with death, and beaten him—that is, God had given me the victory. For I was so young still, so full of life: I could not accept death, as we afterward learn to do, as coming also from God's hand. The first day that my mother came down stairs I sang my jubilate all over the house, and ran about, half laughing, half crying, like a child.

Only for one day. Then began the weary time of convalescence, sometimes better, sometimes worse; the reaction of the household from the excitement of a dangerous illness, which is always trying, and apt to leave folks rather cross. Besides, there were all the purifications to begin at once, with us still in the house. Poor Mrs. Golding! she was very good, more especially when we considered she had lost through us her summer lodgers; for it was now June. Yet for them to come in was as impracticable as for my mother and me to turn out.

"We must make it up to her in some way," said my mother with a sigh, beginning already to trouble herself with domestic and financial anxieties, until she saw that

I would not allow it. I threatened her, if she still persisted in considering me a child, incapable of managing any thing, that I would take the law into my own hands, and treat her like a captive princess—bound in silken chains, but firmly bound. At which she laughed, and said I was "growing clever," besides tyrannical. But I think when Mrs. Golding assured her I really had some sense, and was managing matters almost as well as she herself could, my mother was rather proud than otherwise.

Other things she also, from the feebleness of illness, seemed to have let slip entirely. She scarcely made a single inquiry about my grandfather, or any of them in Bath. This was well, since it might have hurt her to find out—as I accidentally did—that none of them had sent to inquire; not even to the garden gate. But perhaps, on every account, this was best. And yet I could not choose but think it rather strange.

Gradually we passed out of the mysterious, unnatural half-life of the sick-room into the full, clear daylight of common existence. Then we found out what two changed creatures we were in many respects, but still, ever and always, my mother and I.

We were sitting together in the parlor, that is, I was sitting, busy at work, and she lying idle, as was our way now. I had taken very much to my needle—the girl's dislike, the woman's consolation. The doctor had just been, and said our invalid was much better—quite able to see any body, only people were afraid of infection still; and besides there was nobody to come. But he said half the village had inquired for us, and to one person in particular he had had to give or send a bulletin every day.

Only after the doctor had gone there darted into my mind the possibility as to who that person was. To let go of one's friends is one thing, but to be forced to feel that they have let you go, in an unkind way, and that you can not think quite so well of them as you used to do, is another and a much harder trial. As I said my prayers that night, I added earnestly, "Thank God!"—For what—He knew.

But neither that day nor the next did I let my mind wander one minute from my darling mother, given back to me from the very jaws of the grave. Oh, what a girl can be to a mother—a grown-up girl who is gaining the sense and usefulness of womanhood! And oh, what a mother is to a daughter, who now learns fully to feel her value, and gives her all the devotion of a lover and all the duty of a child! More especially if no duty is exacted. My mother and I never even mentioned the word. But I loved her—God knows how I loved her—even then and through it all.

My needle-work done, I took to balancing our weekly accounts, which cost me as much trouble as if I had been Chancellor of the Exchequer, and when they were done, began to tell my mother of a good suggestion of Mrs. Golding's—that we should go to some sea-side lodging she knew of for a week or two, while she got the rooms cleaned and repapered; then we could come back and remain here the whole summer.

"She does not want to part with us; she has grown so fond of you, mother."

"But she will want more rent, and how can we pay?"

"I can pay!" said I, with pride. "I could not tell you till now, darling, but the doctor wants me to teach his children, as soon as ever we are out quarantine. He says, politely, such a good nurse will make a good governess, which does not follow. But I'll try. Do you consent?"

She sighed. She too might have had other dreams; but they had passed away like mine. She accepted the fact that I must be a governess, after all.

We kissed one another, and then, to prevent her dwelling on the subject, I began the innocent, caressing nonsense which one gets into the habit of during sickness, when the patient's mind is too feeble, and the nurse's too full, to take in aught beyond the small interests close at hand. We were silly enough, no doubt, but happy—when I heard a step come up the garden, a step I knew.

My first thought—I can not well tell what it was; my second, that we were still an infected household.

"Stop him!" cried I, starting up and running to the door. "Somebody must stop him. Mrs. Golding, tell that gentleman he is not to come in."

"Why not?" And I saw him stand there, with his kind, smiling face. "Why not, Cousin Elma?"

"Because it is not safe—we are in quarantine still, you know."

"Of course I know—that and every thing else. But I have taken all precautions. Your doctor and I are the best of friends. He sent me here—Mrs. Picardy, may I come in?"

"Certainly," she answered, looking quite pleased; so without more ado he entered. Though he took no notice, I perceived that he saw the change in her—saw it and was very sorry, both for her and me. Appropriating my chair, he sat down beside her and began talking to her, giving small attention to me, beyond a nod and smile. But that was enough; it felt like windows opened and sunshine coming into a long-shut-up room.

"General Picardy sends all sorts of kind messages to you. He left Bath almost directly after your daughter went. He said he could not bear the dullness of the house. But I have kept him almost daily informed of you both."

"Then we were not forsaken by you all?" said my mother gently, by which I guessed she had thought more of the matter than I supposed.

Cousin Conrad shook his head gayly. "Elma, tell your mother she does not quite know us yet—not so well as you do."

She looked up quickly, this dear mother of mine, first at him and then at me; but there was nothing to see. In him, of course nothing; in me— But I had learned to accept his kindness as he meant it, the frank familiar friendship which implied nothing more. I answered Cousin Conrad as I would have answered any other friend whom I warmly liked and respected, and in whom I entirely believed.

Then I took my sewing again, and left him to his chat with my mother, which she evidently enjoyed. He had come to see her so often while I was in Bath, that they were better friends than I knew. My only wonder was that all this long time she had never praised him—scarcely spoken of him to me at all.

He took tea with us, and we were very happy in his company; so happy that I almost forgot to be afraid for him. At last, I thankfully heard him tell my mother that he had had small-pox very severely as a boy, and since then had gone in the way of it many times with perfect impunity.

"Not that I should ever run useless risks—one's self is not the only person to think of; and before I go home I mean to change my clothes and do a deal of fumigation. You need not have the slightest uneasiness about me, Mrs. Picardy. I may come again?"

"We shall be very happy to see you."

There was a little stiffness in my mother's manner, but she looked at him as if she liked him. I knew her face so well.

"Not that I shall burden you with many visits, as I am still going to India, though not just yet. Would you like to hear how things are settled?"

Without any apologies, but telling us as naturally as if we belonged to him, he explained that the hill-station to which he had been ordered was so healthy that the doctor said he would be as well there as in England, perhaps better. Two or three years might re-establish his strength entirely.

"And I should be thankful for that. Though when I first came home I did not much care. At five-and-twenty even, I thought my life was done."

"Mine is not, even at seven-and-forty," said my mother, smiling.

"But then you have your child."

"Aye, I have my child."

My mother looked at me—such a look! As I knelt beside her sofa, laughing, yet within an inch of crying, Cousin Conrad leaned over us and touched my hand. I felt all the blood rush into my face, and my mother saw it.

He stayed but a minute or two longer; I let him out at the gate and listened to the clatter of his horse's hoofs up the village, then came back into the parlor at once.

My mother lay quite still, looking straight before her. In her eyes was a curious expression—not exactly sad, but pensive, as if her mind had wandered far away, and a letter which Cousin Conrad had just given her, saying it was from the General, and he hoped would please her as it had pleased the sender, lay untouched on her lap.

"Shall I open it?" said I, glad to say and do something.

It was a very kind letter, signed by him with his feeble, shaky signature, though the body of it was in another handwriting—one which we both recognized. And it inclosed a hundred-pound note, begging our acceptance of the "trifle" to defray the expenses of her illness, "until I can make permanent provision for my daughter-in-law and her child."

"*Your* child, you see, mother. He puts us both together—he does not want to take me from you now; and if he did, ever so much, I would not go. I will never leave you again—never, darling mother!"

She smiled, but not a word said she—not a single word.

I had expected she would say something of our visitor and his visit, but she did not, until just as we were going to bed, when she asked me to give her my grandfather's letter, as she would like to read it over again.

"It is very kind of him; but I suppose Major Picardy, who seems almost like a son to him, is at the root of it all."

"I suppose so."

"He, too, is very kind. Indeed, I never met any man who seemed to me so thoroughly good, so entirely unselfish, reliable, and true. No one could know him without loving him."

She looked at me—a keen, steady, half-smiling, half-pensive look. From that moment I was quite certain that my mother had found out all.

CHAPTER XIV.

All my life I have been the recipient of countless love-stories, the confidante both of young men and maidens, and I always found the benefit of that sage proverb, "Least said, soonest mended." On my side certainly, because many a silly fancy is fanned into a misplaced love by talking it over with a foolish sympathizer; on theirs, because I have generally found that those who felt the most said the least. Happiness is sometimes loquacious; but to pain — and there is so much pain always mixed up in love affairs—the safest and best panacea is silence.

My mother and I were silent to one another, perfectly silent, though we must have read one another's hearts as clear as a book, day by day; still neither spoke. What was there to speak about? He had never said a word to me that all the world might not hear, and I—I would not think of myself or of my future. Indeed I seemed to have no future at all after the 18th of September, the day on which the ship was to sail from Southampton.

Between now and then our life was full enough, even

though outside it was as quiet and lonely as before I went to Bath, except for one friend who came to see us now and then, like any ordinary friend, to whom our interests were dear, as his to us. He came generally on a Sunday, being so occupied during the week, and he used to call us his "Sunday rest," saying that when he was abroad he would try to console himself for the loss of it by writing regularly "Dominical letters."

He was very cheerful about his departure, and very certain as to his return, which he meant to be, at the latest, within four years.

"Elma will then be one-and-twenty, and you not quite a septuagenarian, Mrs. Picardy, and the General will be only seventy-five. As I told him the other day, when he spoke of my being one day master at Broadlands, it is likely to be a good many years yet before that time arrives."

But he would be master there some time, as of course he and we both knew. Occasionally we all took a dip into the far-away future, planning what he was to do with his wealth and influence—schemes all for others, none for himself. Not a thought of luxury or ease, or worldly position, only how he should best use all the good things that might fall to him so as to do the widest good.

How proud I was of him—and am still!

My mother, I could see, enjoyed his society very much.

She told me once there was in him a charm of manner that she had never seen in any man, except one. "Only," she added, "in nothing else does he at all resemble your father."

Though she said this with a sigh, it was not a sigh of pain. She was in no way unhappy, I think—quite the contrary—only a little meditative and grave, but that chiefly when we were alone. When Cousin Conrad came she received him warmly, and exerted herself to make all things as pleasant to him as possible; the more so, because sometimes I was hardly able to speak a word.

What long, still Sunday afternoons we used to spend, all three together, in our little parlor! What twilight walks we had across the Tyning and over the fields! Cousin Conrad always gave my mother his arm, and I followed after, watching the two, and noticing his exceeding tenderness over her; but I was not jealous of him—not at all.

At first I could see she was a little nervous in his company, inclined to be irritable, and quick to mark any little peculiarities he had—and he had a few; but she never criticised him, only watched him; and gradually I could perceive that she grew satisfied, and neither criticised nor watched him any more.

I had leisure to observe and think over these two, because I dared not think for a moment of myself—how it would be with me when he ceased to come, when we missed him out of our life, and the seas rolled between us, and his familiar presence was only a remembrance and a dream. Many a time when I could not sleep of nights—when all these things came upon me in such a tide that I could have wrung my hands and screamed, or got up and paced the room in the darkness like a wild creature in its cage, only for fear of disturbing my mother—she would put out her hand and feel for me, "Child, are you wide awake still?" and take me silently into her arms.

Her tenderness over me in those last weeks—those last days—I can not describe, but have never ceased to remember. She kept me constantly employed; in fact I was nervously eager after work, though I often left it half finished. But whatever I did or left undone, she never blamed me. She treated me a little like a sick child, but without telling me I was ill. For I was ill—sick unto death at times with misery, with bitter, bitter humiliation—and then by fits unutterably happy; but of the happiness or the misery we neither of us spoke at all.

Only once I remember her telling me, as if by accident, the history of a friend of hers, a girl no older than myself, who when one day coming into a room saw a face which she had never seen before, yet from that moment she loved it—loved it, in one way or other, all her life.

"And he deserved her love; he was a noble and good man," said my mother.

"Did she marry him?"

"No."

We were silent a little, and then my mother continued, sewing busily as she spoke. "The world might say it was a rather sad story, but I do not. I never blamed her; I scarcely even pitied her. Love comes to us, as all other things come, by the will of God; but whether it do good or harm depends, also, like other things apparently, upon our own will. There are such things as broken hearts and blighted lives, but these are generally feeble hearts and selfish lives. The really noble, of men or women, are those who have strength to love, and strength also to endure."

I said nothing, but I never forgot those healing words; and often, when most inclined to despise myself, it was balm to my heart to know that, reading it, as I was quite sure she did, my mother did not despise me; and so I made up my mind, as she had said, to "endure."

What *she* must have endured, for me and through me —often, alas! from me, for I was very irritable at times —no tongue can tell. Mothers only, I think, can understand how vicarious suffering is sometimes the sharpest of all. During those days I used to pity myself; now, looking back upon them, I pity my mother. Yet I have no recollection of her ever changing from that sweet motherly calmness which was the only thing that soothed my pain.

Her pain, the anguish of seeing herself no longer able to make the entire happiness of her child, of watching the power slip out of her hands, and for a while perhaps feeling, with unutterable bitterness, a vague dread that the love is slipping away too—of this I never once thought then; I did afterward.

Well, somehow or other the time went by and brought us to the last week, the last day; which Cousin Conrad asked if he might spend with us, both because "we were the dearest friends he had," and because he had a somewhat important message to bring from my grandfather, with whom he had been staying at Broadlands.

"And a charming place it is," he wrote, "and a very well-managed estate too, though it is in Ireland." It was always a pet joke of his against my mother that she disliked every thing Irish, and distrusted him because he was just a little bit of an Irishman. She used to laugh, saying it was quite true he had all the Irish virtues—the warm, generous heart, the gay spirits, the quick sympathy, the sweet courtesy which would always rather say a kind thing than an unkind one. As for his Irish faults, she declined to pass judgment upon them. Time would show. "Ah, yes," he would sometimes answer, gravely, "if heaven grant me time."

But these passing sadnesses of his I never noticed much; the mere sight of him was enough to make any one glad; and when he came, even though it was his last time of coming, and I knew it, the joy of seeing him after a week's absence was as great as if he had been absent a year, and we had all three forgotten that he was ever to leave us again.

He and my mother fell at once to talking, discussing the proposition of which my grandfather had made him the bearer. This was, that she and I should come at once to live at Broadlands, not, as I at first feared, in the characters of Miss Picardy and Miss Picardy's mother, but that she should take her position as his son's widow and the mistress of his house so long as the General lived.

"That may be many years or few," said Cousin Conrad, "and after his death he promises nothing; but," with a smile, "I think you need not be afraid."

And then he went on to explain that it was my grandfather's wish to spend half the year at Broadlands and the other half in Dublin or London, according as was convenient, especially with reference to me and the completion of my education, so as to fit me for whatever position in society I might be called upon to fill.

"Not that she is ill-educated, or unaccomplished. We know what she is, do we not, Mrs. Picardy? Still her grandfather wishes her to be quite perfect, doubtless with the idea that she shall one day be—" He stopped. "I have no right to say any more, for I know nothing of the General's intentions. All I entreat is—accept his kindness. It will prove a blessing to himself, and to you also. Elma rich will be a much more useful woman than Elma poor. This, whether she marry or not. If she should marry, and I hope she will one day—"

Here my mother looked up sharply. There was in her face a slight shade of annoyance, even displeasure; but it met his—so sad, so calm, so resolute—and passed away. She said nothing, only sighed.

"Forgive my referring to this subject, Mrs. Picardy; but it is one upon which the General feels very strongly; indeed, he bade me speak of it, both to relieve your mind and your daughter's. There was once a gentleman, a Sir Thomas Appleton—Elma may have told you about him."

No. Elma had not. I felt I was expected to speak; so I said with a strange composure, and yet not strange, for it seemed as if I were past feeling any thing now, "that I had not thought it worth while to trouble my mother with my trouble about Sir Thomas Appleton."

"Trouble is an odd word for a young lady to use when a young man falls in love with her," said Cousin Conrad, smiling; "but she really was very miserable. She looked the picture of despair for days. Never mind! as Mercutio says, 'Men have died and worms have eaten them, but not for love.' Sir Thomas is not dead yet—not likely to die. And your grandfather bade me assure you, Elma, that if half-a-dozen Sir Thomases should appear, he will not urge you to marry one of them unless you choose."

"That is right," said my mother, "and Elma was quite right too. If she do not love a man, she must never marry him, however her friends might wish it. She will not be unhappy even if she never marry at all. My dear child!"

"Yes, you say truly," answered Cousin Conrad, after a long pause, "and truly, also, you call her 'a child.' Therefore, as I told the General, before she marries, or is even engaged, she ought to have plenty of opportunity of seeing all kinds of men—good men—and of choosing deliberately, when she does choose, so that she may never regret it afterward. Sometimes in their twenties girls feel differently from what they do in their teens, and if after being bound they wake up and wish themselves free again—God forbid such a misfortune should happen to her."

"It never will, I think," said my mother.

"It never must," said Cousin Conrad, decisively. "We will guard against the remotest chance of such a thing. She shall be left quite free; her mother will be constantly beside her; she will have every opportunity of choice; and when she does choose, among the many who are sure to love her, she will do it with her eyes open. You understand me, do you not—you at least?" added he, very earnestly.

"I think I do."

"And you forgive me? Remember, I am going away."

"I do remember. I am not likely ever to forget," replied my mother, visibly affected, and offering him her hand. He clasped it warmly, and turned away, not saying another word.

For me, I sat apart, thinking not much of what either of them said or did; though afterward I recalled it all. Thinking, indeed, very little about any thing beyond the one fact—that he was going away, that after this day I should see him no more for days and weeks and months and years.

I sat apart, taking no share in the conversation, only watching him by stealth, him to whom I was nothing at all, and he nothing to me, except just my Cousin Conrad. Yet then, aye, and at any time in my life, I could have died for him!—said not a word, but just quietly died! I sat, trying to lay up in my heart every trick of his manner, every line of his face, as a sort of memorial storehouse to live upon during the dark famine days that were coming.

"Well, then, that business is settled," said he, with a sigh of relief. "You will go to Broadlands as soon as you can—perhaps even next week;" and he proceeded to give minute directions for our journey, saying it would be a comfort for him to know that all was arranged as easily as possible, and he would think of us safe in my grandfather's beautiful home, while he was tossing on the Bay of Biscay. He could not hear of us for many months. There was no overland route to India then.

"But I can wait. I have learned to wait, and yet it sometimes seems a little hard, at thirty-six years old. But it is right—it is right," he added, half to himself. Years after how thankful I was to remember his words!

Then, rising, he suggested that we should sit talking no longer; but all three go out together into the pleasant afternoon sunshine and "enjoy ourselves."

"Enjoy" seemed a strange word to use, and yet it was a true one. When friends are all at peace together, with entire trust and content in one another, there is no bitterness even in the midst of parting pain. And such was his sweet nature, and the influence it had upon those about him, that this fact was especially remarkable. I have now not a single recollection of that day which is not pleasant as well as dear.

We spent part of it at a place where my mother and I had often talked of going, the abbey which we had started to see that afternoon when the bleak wind made me resolve to buy her a Paisley shawl. As we again crossed the Tyning, I overheard her telling Cousin Conrad the whole story.

"Just like her—just like Elma!" said he, turning round to look at me, and then told how on his side he remembered the General's calling him into his room to write a letter concerning the possible granddaughter which he thought he had found.

"It is strange upon what small chances great things seem to hang. We go on and on, year after year, and nothing happens, and we think nothing ever will happen; and then, suddenly turning a corner, we come upon our destiny. Is it not so, Mrs. Picardy?"

I do not remember what my mother answered, or if she answered at all. She was exceedingly kind, even tender to him; but she was also exceedingly grave.

Thus we wandered on till we reached the old abbey—a mere ruin, and little cared for by the owners of the house in whose grounds it stood. The refectory was used as a wood-shed, the chapel as a stable, and above it, ascended by a broken stair, were two large rooms, still in good preservation, said to have been the monks' library and their dove-cot.

"You can still see the holes in the stone walls, I am told, where the pigeons built their nests," said my mother. "Go up and look at them, if you like, you two; I will rest here."

She sat down on a heap of hay, and we went on without her. Only once she called after us that the stair was dangerous, and he must take care of "the child."

"Ah, yes!" he said with such a smile! It made me quite cheerful, and we began examining every thing and discussing every thing quite after the old way. Then we rested a while, and stood looking out through the narrow slits of windows onto the pleasant country beyond.

"What a comfortable life those old monks must have made for themselves! And how curious it must have been as they sat poring over their manuscript-writing or illuminating in this very room, to hear close by the innocent little pigeons cooing in their nests! I wonder if they ever thought that the poor little birds were, in some things, happier far than they."

"How?" said I, and then instinctively guessed, and wished I had not said it.

"Very jolly old fellows, though, they must have been, with a great idea of making themselves comfortable. See, Elma, that must be the remains of their orchard—those gnarled apple-trees, so very old, yet trying to bear a few apples still; and there are their fish-ponds—undoubtedly you always find fish-ponds near monasteries; and look, what a splendid avenue of walnut-trees! No doubt they had all the good things of this life; except one, the best thing of all—home; a married home."

It was only a word—but oh! the tone in which he said it! he who, he once told me, had never had a home in all his life. Did he regret it? Was he, as I always fancied when he looked sad—was he thinking of Agnes? Only Agnes?

I was not clever, and I was very young; but I believe, even then, if any one had wanted it, I could have learned how to make a home, a real home, as only a loving woman can. Not a wealthy home, maybe, and one that might have had its fair proportion of cares and anxieties; but I would have struggled through them all. I would not have been afraid of any thing. I would have fought with and conquered, please God, all remediable evils; and those I could not conquer I would have sat down and endured without complaining. No one need have been afraid that I had not strength enough to bear my own burden, perhaps the burden of two. Nay, it would have made me happier. I never wished to have an easy life; only a life with love in it —love and trust. Oh! how happy I could have been, however difficult my lot, if only I had had some one always beside me, some one whom I could at once look up to and take care of, cherish and adore! How we could have spent our lives together, have passed through poverty if need be, and risen joyfully to prosperity, still together! have shared our prime and our decline, always together! Instead of this—

No! Silence, my heart! What am I that I should fight against God? It was his will. With him there are no such words as "might have been."

One thing I remember vividly—that as we stood there, looking out, Cousin Conrad put his hand a moment lightly on my shoulder.

"Keep as you are a minute. Sometimes as you stand thus, with your profile turned away, you look so very like her—so like Agnes—that I could fancy it was she herself come back again, young as ever, while I have grown quite old. Yes, compared with you, Elma, I am quite old."

I said nothing. If I had said any thing—if I could have told him that those we love to us never seem old, that even had it been as he said, he, with his gray hair, was more to me, and would be, down to the most helpless old age, than all the young men in the world. But how could I have said it? And if I had, it would have made no difference. Years afterward I recalled his look—firm and sweet, never wavering in a purpose which he thought right. No; nothing would have made any difference.

We stayed a few minutes longer, and then came back, he helping me tenderly down the broken stairs, to my mother's side. She gave a start, and a sudden eager, anxious look at us both; but when Cousin Conrad said in his usual voice that it was time for us to go home, she looked down again and—sighed.

We went home, rather silently now, and took a hasty tea, for he had to be back in Bath by a certain hour, and

"Cousin Conrad put his hand a moment lightly on my shoulder."

besides, the mists were gathering, and my mother urged him to avoid the risk of a cold night-ride.

"We must say good-by at last, and perhaps it is best after all to say it quickly," I heard her tell him in an undertone. Her voice trembled, the tears stood in her eyes. For me, I never stirred or wept. I was as still as a stone.

"You are right," answered he, rising. "Good-by, and God bless you. That is all one needs to say." Taking her hand, he kissed it. Then, glancing at me, he asked her—my mother only—"May I?"

She bent her head in assent. Crossing the room, he came and kissed me, once on my forehead, and once—oh, thank God, just that once!—on my mouth. Where I keep it—that kiss of his—till I can give it back to him in Paradise.

For in this world I never saw my Cousin Conrad more.

* * * * *

We had a very happy three years—my mother and I—as happy as we had ever known. For after Cousin Conrad's departure we seemed to close up together—she and I—in one another's loving arms; understanding one another thoroughly, though still, as ever, we did not speak one word about him that all the world might not have heard.

Outwardly, our life was wholly free from care. We

had as much of each other's society, or nearly as much, as we had ever had, with the cares of poverty entirely removed. My grandfather proved as good as his word, and all that Cousin Conrad had said of him he justified to the full. He received my mother with cordial welcome, and treated her from first to last with unfailing respect and consideration. She had every luxury that I could desire for her, and she needed luxuries, for after her illness she was never her strong, active self again. But she was her dear self always—the sweetest, brightest little mother in all the world.

To the world itself, however, we were two very grand people — Mrs. and Miss Picardy of Broadlands. At which we often laughed between ourselves, knowing that we were in reality exactly the same as in our shut-up poverty days—just "my mother and I."

Cousin Conrad's letters were our great enjoyment. He never missed a single mail. Generally he wrote to her, with a little note inside for me, inquiring about my studies and amusements, and telling me of his own; though of himself personally he said very little. Whether he were well or ill, happy or miserable, we could guess only by indirect evidence. But one thing was clear enough—his intense longing to be at home.

"Not a day shall I wait," he said in a letter to my grandfather—"not a single day after the term of absence I have prescribed to myself is ended." And my grandfather coughed, saying mysteriously that "Conrad always had his crotchets;" he hoped this would be the last of them; it was not so very long to look forward.

Did I look forward? Had I any dreams of a possible future? I can not tell. My life was so full and busy — my mother seemed obstinately determined to keep it busy—that I had little time for dreams.

She took me out into society, and I think both she and my grandfather enjoyed society's receiving me well. I believe I made what is called a "sensation" in both Dublin and London. I was even presented at Court, and the young Queen said a kind word or two about me, in Her Majesty's own pleasant way. Well, well, all that is gone by now; but at the time I enjoyed it. It was good to be worth something—even to look at—and I liked to be liked very much, until some few did rather more than like me, and then I was sometimes very unhappy. But my grandfather kept his promise; he never urged upon me any offer of marriage. And my mother, too—my tender mother—asked me not a single question as to the why and the wherefore, though, one after another, I persistently refused them all.

"When she is one-and-twenty, my dear, we may hope she will decide. By then she will have time to know her own mind. Conrad said so, and Conrad is always right."

Thus said my grandfather to my mother, and they

both smiled at one another; they were the best friends now, and so they remained to the last.

The last came sooner than any of us had thought —for Cousin Conrad's prophecies were not realized. When we had had only three years in which to make him happy—and I know we did make him happy—my dear grandfather died: suddenly, painlessly, without even having had time to bid us good-by. It was a great shock, and we mourned for him as if we had loved him all our lives. Aye, even though, to the great surprise of our affectionate friends—a large circle now—he left us only a small annuity—the rest of his fortune going, as the will proved he had always meant it to go, to Cousin Conrad. I was so glad!

Cousin Conrad was now obliged to come home. We had only one line from him, when he got the sad news, begging my mother to remain mistress at Broadlands until he arrived there, and adding that, if it did not trouble us very much, he should be grateful could we manage to meet him at Southampton, he being "rather an invalid."

So we went. I need not say any thing about the journey. When it ended, my mother, just at the last minute, proposed that I should remain in the carriage, at the dock gates, while she went forward to the ship's side, where we could dimly perceive a crowd disembarking.

They disembarked. I saw them land in happy groups, with equally happy friends to greet them, laughing and crying and kissing one another. They all came home, safe and sound, all but one—*my* one. Deep in the Red Sea, where the busy ships sail over him, and the warm waves rock him in his sleep, they had left him—as much as could die of him—my Cousin Conrad.

* * * * * *

He had died of the fatal family disease which he knew he was doomed to, though the warm climate of the East and the pure air of the hills kept it dormant for a long time. But some accidental exposure brought on inflammation of his lungs; after which he began to sink rapidly. The doctors told him he would never reach England alive; but he was determined to try. I heard it was wonderful how long the brave spirit upbore the feeble body. He did not suffer much, but just lay every day on deck; alone, quite alone, as far as near friends went—yet watched and tended by all the passengers, as if he had belonged to them for years. In the midst of them all, these kind, strange faces, he one day suddenly, when no one expected it, "fell on sleep." For he looked as if asleep—they said—with the sun shining on his face, and his hands folded, as quiet as a child.

All that was his became mine. He left it me—and it was a large fortune—in a brief will, made hastily the very day after he had received the tidings of my grandfather's death. He gave me every thing absolutely, both "because it was my right," and "because he had always loved me."

He had always loved me. Then, why grieve?

In course of years, I think I have almost ceased to grieve. If, long ago, merely because I loved him, I had felt as if already married, how much more so now, when nothing could ever happen to change this feeling, or make my love for him a sin?

I do not say there was not an intermediate and terrible time, a time of utter blankness and darkness, when I "walked through the valley of the shadow of death;" alone, quite alone. But by-and-by I came out of it into the safe twilight—*we* came out of it, I should say, for she had been close beside me all the while, my dearest mother!

She helped me to carry out my life; as like his as I could make it, in the way I knew he would most approve. And, so doing, it has not been by any means an unhappy life. I have had his wealth to accomplish all his schemes of benevolence; I have sought out his friends and made them mine, and been as true to them as he would have been. In short, I have tried to do all that he was obliged to leave undone, and to make myself contented in the doing of it.

"Contented," I think, was the word people most often

used concerning us during the many peaceful years we spent together, my mother and I. Now it is only I. But I am, I think, a contented old woman yet. My own are still my own—perhaps the more so as I approach the time of reunion. For even here, to those who live in it and understand what it means, there is, both for us and for our dead, both in this life and in the life to come, the same "kingdom of heaven."

Of course, I have always remained Elma Picardy.

THE END.

ANNUAL RECORD OF SCIENCE AND INDUSTRY FOR 1872. Edited by Prof. SPENCER F. BAIRD, of the Smithsonian Institution, with the Assistance of Eminent Men of Science. 12mo, over 700 pp., Cloth, $2 00. (Uniform with the *Annual Record of Science and Industry for* 1871. 12mo, Cloth, $2 00.)

COL. FORNEY'S ANECDOTES OF PUBLIC MEN. Anecdotes of Public Men. By JOHN W. FORNEY. 12mo, Cloth, $2 00.

MISS BEECHER'S HOUSEKEEPER AND HEALTHKEEPER: Containing Five Hundred Recipes for Economical and Healthful Cooking; also, many Directions for securing Health and Happiness. Approved by Physicians of all Classes. Illustrations. 12mo, Cloth, $1 50.

FARM BALLADS. By WILL CARLETON. Handsomely Illustrated. Square 8vo, Ornamental Cloth, $2 00; Gilt Edges, $2 50.

POETS OF THE NINETEENTH CENTURY. The Poets of the Nineteenth Century. Selected and Edited by the Rev. ROBERT ARIS WILLMOTT. With English and American Additions, arranged by EVERT A. DUYCKINCK, Editor of "Cyclopædia of American Literature." Comprising Selections from the Greatest Authors of the Age. Superbly Illustrated with 141 Engravings from Designs by the most Eminent Artists. In elegant small 4to form, printed on Superfine Tinted Paper, richly bound in extra Cloth, Beveled, Gilt Edges, $5 00; Half Calf, $5 50; Full Turkey Morocco, $9 00.

THE REVISION OF THE ENGLISH VERSION OF THE NEW TESTAMENT. With an Introduction by the Rev. P. SCHAFF, D.D. 618 pp., Crown 8vo, Cloth, $3 00.

This work embraces in one volume:

I. ON A FRESH REVISION OF THE ENGLISH NEW TESTAMENT. By J. B. LIGHTFOOT, D.D., Canon of St. Paul's, and Hulsean Professor of Divinity, Cambridge. Second Edition, Revised. 196 pp.

II. ON THE AUTHORIZED VERSION OF THE NEW TESTAMENT in Connection with some Recent Proposals for its Revision. By RICHARD CHENEVIX TRENCH, D.D., Archbishop of Dublin. 194 pp.

III. CONSIDERATIONS ON THE REVISION OF THE ENGLISH VERSION OF THE NEW TESTAMENT. By C. J. ELLICOTT, D.D., Bishop of Gloucester and Bristol. 178 pp.

NORDHOFF'S CALIFORNIA. California: For Health, Pleasure, and Residence. A Book for Travelers and Settlers. Illustrated. 8vo, Paper, $2 00; Cloth, $2 50.

MOTLEY'S DUTCH REPUBLIC. The Rise of the Dutch Republic. By JOHN LOTHROP MOTLEY, LL.D., D.C.L. With a Portrait of William of Orange. 3 vols., 8vo, Cloth, $10 50.

MOTLEY'S UNITED NETHERLANDS. History of the United Netherlands: from the Death of William the Silent to the Twelve Years' Truce—1609. With a full View of the English-Dutch Struggle against Spain, and of the Origin and Destruction of the Spanish Armada. By JOHN LOTHROP MOTLEY, LL.D., D.C.L. Portraits. 4 vols., 8vo, Cloth, $14 00.

NAPOLEON'S LIFE OF CÆSAR. The History of Julius Cæsar. By His late Imperial Majesty NAPOLEON III. Two Volumes ready. Library Edition, 8vo, Cloth, $3 50 per vol.

HAYDN'S DICTIONARY OF DATES, relating to all Ages and Nations. For Universal Reference. Edited by BENJAMIN VINCENT, Assistant Secretary and Keeper of the Library of the Royal Institution of Great Britain; and Revised for the Use of American Readers. 8vo, Cloth, $5 00; Sheep, $6 00.

MACGREGOR'S ROB ROY ON THE JORDAN. The Rob Roy on the Jordan, Nile, Red Sea, and Gennesareth, &c. A Canoe Cruise in Palestine and Egypt, and the Waters of Damascus. By J. MACGREGOR, M.A. With Maps and Illustrations. Crown 8vo, Cloth, $2 50.

WALLACE'S MALAY ARCHIPELAGO. The Malay Archipelago: the Land of the Orang-Utan and the Bird of Paradise. A Narrative of Travel, 1854-1862. With Studies of Man and Nature. By ALFRED RUSSEL WALLACE. With Ten Maps and Fifty-one Elegant Illustrations. Crown 8vo, Cloth, $2 50.

WHYMPER'S ALASKA. Travel and Adventure in the Territory of Alaska, formerly Russian America—now Ceded to the United States—and in various other parts of the North Pacific. By FREDERICK WHYMPER. With Map and Illustrations. Crown 8vo, Cloth, $2 50.

ORTON'S ANDES AND THE AMAZON. The Andes and the Amazon; or, Across the Continent of South America. By JAMES ORTON, M.A., Professor of Natural History in Vassar College, Poughkeepsie, N. Y., and Corresponding Member of the Academy of Natural Sciences, Philadelphia. With a New Map of Equatorial America and numerous Illustrations. Crown 8vo, Cloth, $2 00.

WINCHELL'S SKETCHES OF CREATION. Sketches of Creation: a Popular View of some of the Grand Conclusions of the Sciences in reference to the History of Matter and of Life. Together with a Statement of the Intimations of Science respecting the Primordial Condition and the Ultimate Destiny of the Earth and the Solar System. By ALEXANDER WINCHELL, LL.D., Chancellor of the Syracuse University. With Illustrations. 12mo, Cloth, $2 00.

WHITE'S MASSACRE OF ST. BARTHOLOMEW. The Massacre of St. Bartholomew: Preceded by a History of the Religious Wars in the Reign of Charles IX. By HENRY WHITE, M.A. With Illustrations. 8vo, Cloth, $1 75.

LOSSING'S FIELD-BOOK OF THE REVOLUTION. Pictorial Field-Book of the Revolution; or, Illustrations, by Pen and Pencil, of the History, Biography, Scenery, Relics, and Traditions of the War for Independence. By BENSON J. LOSSING. 2 vols., 8vo, Cloth, $14 00; Sheep, $15 00; Half Calf, $18 00; Full Turkey Morocco, $22 00.

LOSSING'S FIELD-BOOK OF THE WAR OF 1812. Pictorial Field-Book of the War of 1812; or, Illustrations, by Pen and Pencil, of the History, Biography, Scenery, Relics, and Traditions of the Last War for American Independence. By BENSON J. LOSSING. With several hundred Engravings on Wood, by Lossing and Barritt, chiefly from Original Sketches by the Author. 1088 pages, 8vo, Cloth, $7 00; Sheep, $8 50; Half Calf, $10 00.

ALFORD'S GREEK TESTAMENT. The Greek Testament: with a critically revised Text; a Digest of Various Readings; Marginal References to Verbal and Idiomatic Usage; Prolegomena; and a Critical and Exegetical Commentary. For the Use of Theological Students and Ministers. By HENRY ALFORD, D.D., Dean of Canterbury. Vol. I., containing the Four Gospels. 944 pages, 8vo, Cloth, $6 00; Sheep, $6 50.

ABBOTT'S FREDERICK THE GREAT. The History of Frederick the Second, called Frederick the Great. By JOHN S. C. ABBOTT. Elegantly Illustrated. 8vo, Cloth, $5 00.

ABBOTT'S HISTORY OF THE FRENCH REVOLUTION. The French Revolution of 1789, as viewed in the Light of Republican Institutions. By JOHN S. C. ABBOTT. With 100 Engravings. 8vo, Cloth, $5 00.

ABBOTT'S NAPOLEON BONAPARTE. The History of Napoleon Bonaparte. By JOHN S. C. ABBOTT. With Maps, Woodcuts, and Portraits on Steel. 2 vols., 8vo, Cloth, $10 00.

ABBOTT'S NAPOLEON AT ST. HELENA; or, Interesting Anecdotes and Remarkable Conversations of the Emperor during the Five and a Half Years of his Captivity. Collected from the Memorials of Las Casas, O'Meara, Montholon, Antommarchi, and others. By JOHN S. C. ABBOTT. With Illustrations. 8vo, Cloth, $5 00.

ADDISON'S COMPLETE WORKS. The Works of Joseph Addison, embracing the whole of the "Spectator." Complete in 3 vols., 8vo, Cloth, $6 00.

ALCOCK'S JAPAN. The Capital of the Tycoon: a Narrative of a Three Years' Residence in Japan. By Sir RUTHERFORD ALCOCK, K.C.B., Her Majesty's Envoy Extraordinary and Minister Plenipotentiary in Japan. With Maps and Engravings. 2 vols., 12mo, Cloth, $3 50.

ALISON'S HISTORY OF EUROPE. FIRST SERIES: From the Commencement of the French Revolution, in 1789, to the Restoration of the Bourbons, in 1815. [In addition to the Notes on Chapter LXXVI., which correct the errors of the original work concerning the United States, a copious Analytical Index has been appended to this American Edition.] SECOND SERIES: From the Fall of Napoleon, in 1815, to the Accession of Louis Napoleon, in 1852. 8 vols., 8vo, Cloth, $16 00.

BARTH'S NORTH AND CENTRAL AFRICA. Travels and Discoveries in North and Central Africa: being a Journal of an Expedition undertaken under the Auspices of H.B.M.'s Government, in the Years 1849-1855. By HENRY BARTH, Ph.D., D.C.L. Illustrated. 3 vols., 8vo, Cloth, $12 00.

HENRY WARD BEECHER'S SERMONS. Sermons by HENRY WARD BEECHER, Plymouth Church, Brooklyn. Selected from Published and Unpublished Discourses, and Revised by their Author. With Steel Portrait. Complete in 2 vols., 8vo, Cloth, $5 00.

LYMAN BEECHER'S AUTOBIOGRAPHY, &c. Autobiography, Correspondence, &c., of Lyman Beecher, D.D. Edited by his Son, CHARLES BEECHER. With Three Steel Portraits, and Engravings on Wood. In 2 vols., 12mo, Cloth, $5 00.

BOSWELL'S JOHNSON. The Life of Samuel Johnson, LL.D. Including a Journey to the Hebrides. By JAMES BOSWELL, Esq. A New Edition, with numerous Additions and Notes. By JOHN WILSON CROKER, LL.D., F.R.S. Portrait of Boswell. 2 vols., 8vo, Cloth, $4 00.

DRAPER'S CIVIL WAR. History of the American Civil War. By JOHN W. DRAPER, M.D., LL.D., Professor of Chemistry and Physiology in the University of New York. In Three Vols. 8vo, Cloth, $3 50 per vol.

DRAPER'S INTELLECTUAL DEVELOPMENT OF EUROPE. A History of the Intellectual Development of Europe. By JOHN W. DRAPER, M.D., LL.D., Professor of Chemistry and Physiology in the University of New York. 8vo, Cloth, $5 00.

DRAPER'S AMERICAN CIVIL POLICY. Thoughts on the Future Civil Policy of America. By JOHN W. DRAPER, M.D., LL.D., Professor of Chemistry and Physiology in the University of New York. Crown 8vo, Cloth, $2 50.

DU CHAILLU'S AFRICA. Explorations and Adventures in Equatorial Africa, with Accounts of the Manners and Customs of the People, and of the Chase of the Gorilla, the Crocodile, Leopard, Elephant, Hippopotamus, and other Animals. By PAUL B. DU CHAILLU. Numerous Illustrations. 8vo, Cloth, $5 00.

DU CHAILLU'S ASHANGO LAND. A Journey to Ashango Land: and Further Penetration into Equatorial Africa. By PAUL B. DU CHAILLU. New Edition. Handsomely Illustrated. 8vo, Cloth, $5 00.

BELLOWS'S OLD WORLD. The Old World in its New Face: Impressions of Europe in 1867-1868. By HENRY W. BELLOWS. 2 vols., 12mo, Cloth, $3 50.

BRODHEAD'S HISTORY OF NEW YORK. History of the State of New York. By JOHN ROMEYN BRODHEAD. 1609-1691. 2 vols. 8vo, Cloth, $3 00 per vol.

BROUGHAM'S AUTOBIOGRAPHY. Life and Times of HENRY, LORD BROUGHAM. Written by Himself. In Three Volumes. 12mo, Cloth, $2 00 per vol.

BULWER'S PROSE WORKS. Miscellaneous Prose Works of Edward Bulwer, Lord Lytton. 2 vols., 12mo, Cloth, $3 50.

BULWER'S HORACE. The Odes and Epodes of Horace. A Metrical Translation into English. With Introduction and Commentaries. By LORD LYTTON. With Latin Text from the Editions of Orelli, Macleane, and Yonge. 12mo, Cloth, $1 75.

BULWER'S KING ARTHUR, A Poem. By LORD LYTTON. New Edition. 12mo, Cloth, $1 75.

BURNS'S LIFE AND WORKS. The Life and Works of Robert Burns. Edited by ROBERT CHAMBERS. 4 vols., 12mo, Cloth, $6 00.

REINDEER, DOGS, AND SNOW-SHOES. A Journal of Siberian Travel and Explorations made in the Years 1865–'67. By RICHARD J. BUSH, late of the Russo-American Telegraph Expedition. Illustrated. Crown 8vo, Cloth, $3 00.

CARLYLE'S FREDERICK THE GREAT. History of Friedrich II., called Frederick the Great. By THOMAS CARLYLE. Portraits, Maps, Plans, &c. 6 vols., 12mo, Cloth, $12 00.

CARLYLE'S FRENCH REVOLUTION. History of the French Revolution. 2 vols., 12mo, Cloth, $3 50.

CARLYLE'S OLIVER CROMWELL. Letters and Speeches of Oliver Cromwell. With Elucidations and Connecting Narrative. 2 vols., 12mo, Cloth, $3 50.

CHALMERS'S POSTHUMOUS WORKS. The Posthumous Works of Dr. Chalmers. Edited by his Son-in-Law, Rev. WILLIAM HANNA, LL.D. Complete in 9 vols., 12mo, Cloth, $13 50.

COLERIDGE'S COMPLETE WORKS. The Complete Works of Samuel Taylor Coleridge. With an Introductory Essay upon his Philosophical and Theological Opinions. Edited by Professor SHEDD. Complete in Seven Vols. With a Portrait. Small 8vo, Cloth, $10 50.

DOOLITTLE'S CHINA. Social Life of the Chinese: with some Account of their Religious, Governmental, Educational, and Business Customs and Opinions. With special but not exclusive Reference to Fuhchau. By Rev. JUSTUS DOOLITTLE, Fourteen Years Member of the Fuhchau Mission of the American Board. Illustrated with more that 150 characteristic Engravings on Wood. 2 vols., 12mo, Cloth, $5 00.

GIBBON'S ROME. History of the Decline and Fall of the Roman Empire. By EDWARD GIBBON. With Notes by Rev. H. H. MILMAN and M. GUIZOT. A new cheap Edition. To which is added a complete Index of the whole Work, and a Portrait of the Author. 6 vols., 12mo, Cloth, $9 00.

HAZEN'S SCHOOL AND ARMY IN GERMANY AND FRANCE. The School and the Army in Germany and France, with a Diary of Siege Life at Versailles. By Brevet Major-General W. B. HAZEN, U.S.A., Colonel Sixth Infantry. Crown 8vo, Cloth, $2 50.

HARPER'S NEW CLASSICAL LIBRARY. Literal Translations.

The following Vols. are now ready. 12mo, Cloth, $1 50 each.

CÆSAR.—VIRGIL.—SALLUST.—HORACE.—CICERO'S ORATIONS.—CICERO'S OFFICES, &c.—CICERO ON ORATORY AND ORATORS.—TACITUS (2 vols.).—TERENCE.—SOPHOCLES.—JUVENAL.—XENOPHON.—HOMER'S ILIAD.—HOMER'S ODYSSEY.—HERODOTUS.—DEMOSTHENES.—THUCYDIDES.—ÆSCHYLUS.—EURIPIDES (2 vols.).—LIVY (2 vols.).

DAVIS'S CARTHAGE. Carthage and her Remains: being an Account of the Excavations and Researches on the Site of the Phœnician Metropolis in Africa and other adjacent Places. Conducted under the Auspices of Her Majesty's Government. By Dr. DAVIS, F.R.G.S. Profusely Illustrated with Maps, Woodcuts, Chromo-Lithographs, &c. 8vo, Cloth, $4 00.

EDGEWORTH'S (MISS) NOVELS. With Engravings. 10 vols., 12mo, Cloth, $15 00.

GROTE'S HISTORY OF GREECE. 12 vols., 12mo, Cloth, $18 00.

HELPS'S SPANISH CONQUEST. The Spanish Conquest in America, and its Relation to the History of Slavery and to the Government of Colonies. By ARTHUR HELPS. 4 vols., 12mo, Cloth, $6 00.

HALE'S (MRS.) WOMAN'S RECORD. Woman's Record; or, Biographical Sketches of all Distinguished Women, from the Creation to the Present Time. Arranged in Four Eras, with Selections from Female Writers of Each Era. By Mrs. SARAH JOSEPHA HALE. Illustrated with more than 200 Portraits. 8vo, Cloth, $5 00.

HALL'S ARCTIC RESEARCHES. Arctic Researches and Life among the Esquimaux: being the Narrative of an Expedition in Search of Sir John Franklin, in the Years 1860, 1861, and 1862. By CHARLES FRANCIS HALL. With Maps and 100 Illustrations. The Illustrations are from the Original Drawings by Charles Parsons, Henry L. Stephens, Solomon Eytinge, W. S. L. Jewett, and Granville Perkins, after Sketches by Captain Hall. 8vo, Cloth, $5 00.

HALLAM'S CONSTITUTIONAL HISTORY OF ENGLAND, from the Accession of Henry VII. to the Death of George II. 8vo, Cloth, $2 00.

HALLAM'S LITERATURE. Introduction to the Literature of Europe during the Fifteenth, Sixteenth, and Seventeenth Centuries. By HENRY HALLAM. 2 vols., 8vo, Cloth, $4 00.

HALLAM'S MIDDLE AGES. State of Europe during the Middle Ages. By HENRY HALLAM. 8vo, Cloth, $2 00.

HILDRETH'S HISTORY OF THE UNITED STATES. FIRST SERIES: From the First Settlement of the Country to the Adoption of the Federal Constitution. SECOND SERIES: From the Adoption of the Federal Constitution to the End of the Sixteenth Congress. 6 vols., 8vo, Cloth, $18 00.

HUME'S HISTORY OF ENGLAND. History of England, from the Invasion of Julius Cæsar to the Abdication of James II., 1688. By DAVID HUME. A new Edition, with the Author's last Corrections and Improvements. To which is Prefixed a short Account of his Life, written by Himself. With a Portrait of the Author. 6 vols., 12mo, Cloth, $9 00.

JAY'S WORKS. Complete Works of Rev. William Jay: comprising his Sermons, Family Discourses, Morning and Evening Exercises for every Day in the Year, Family Prayers, &c. Author's enlarged Edition, revised. 3 vols., 8vo, Cloth, $6 00.

JEFFERSON'S DOMESTIC LIFE. The Domestic Life of Thomas Jefferson: compiled from Family Letters and Reminiscences, by his Great-Granddaughter, SARAH N. RANDOLPH. With Illustrations. Crown 8vo, Illuminated Cloth, Beveled Edges, $2 50.

JOHNSON'S COMPLETE WORKS. The Works of Samuel Johnson, LL.D. With an Essay on his Life and Genius, by ARTHUR MURPHY, Esq. Portrait of Johnson. 2 vols., 8vo, Cloth, $4 00.

KINGLAKE'S CRIMEAN WAR. The Invasion of the Crimea, and an Account of its Progress down to the Death of Lord Raglan. By ALEXANDER WILLIAM KINGLAKE. With Maps and Plans. Two Vols. ready. 12mo, Cloth, $2 00 per vol.

KINGSLEY'S WEST INDIES. At Last: A Christmas in the West Indies. By CHARLES KINGSLEY. Illustrated. 12mo, Cloth, $1 50.

KRUMMACHER'S DAVID, KING OF ISRAEL. David, the King of Israel: a Portrait drawn from Bible History and the Book of Psalms. By FREDERICK WILLIAM KRUMMACHER, D.D., Author of "Elijah the Tishbite," &c. Translated under the express Sanction of the Author by the Rev. M. G. EASTON, M.A. With a Letter from Dr. Krummacher to his American Readers, and a Portrait. 12mo, Cloth, $1 75.

LAMB'S COMPLETE WORKS. The Works of Charles Lamb. Comprising his Letters, Poems, Essays of Elia, Essays upon Shakspeare, Hogarth, &c., and a Sketch of his Life, with the Final Memorials, by T. NOON TALFOURD. Portrait. 2 vols., 12mo, Cloth, $3 00.

LIVINGSTONE'S SOUTH AFRICA. Missionary Travels and Researches in South Africa; including a Sketch of Sixteen Years' Residence in the Interior of Africa, and a Journey from the Cape of Good Hope to Loando on the West Coast; thence across the Continent, down the River Zambesi, to the Eastern Ocean. By DAVID LIVINGSTONE, LL.D., D.C.L. With Portrait, Maps by Arrowsmith, and numerous Illustrations. 8vo, Cloth, $4 50.

LIVINGSTONES' ZAMBESI. Narrative of an Expedition to the Zambesi and its Tributaries, and of the Discovery of the Lakes Shirwa and Nyassa. 1858-1864. By DAVID and CHARLES LIVINGSTONE. With Map and Illustrations. 8vo, Cloth, $5 00.

M'CLINTOCK & STRONG'S CYCLOPÆDIA. Cyclopædia of Biblical, Theological, and Ecclesiastical Literature. Prepared by the Rev. JOHN M'CLINTOCK, D.D., and JAMES STRONG, S.T.D. *5 vols. now ready.* Royal 8vo, Price per vol., Cloth, $5 00; Sheep, $6 00; Half Morocco, $8 00.

MARCY'S ARMY LIFE ON THE BORDER. Thirty Years of Army Life on the Border. Comprising descriptions of the Indian Nomads of the Plains; Explorations of New Territory; a Trip across the Rocky Mountains in the Winter; Descriptions of the Habits of Different Animals found in the West, and the Methods of Hunting them; with Incidents in the Life of Different Frontier Men, &c., &c. By Brevet Brigadier-General R. B. MARCY, U.S.A., Author of "The Prairie Traveller." With numerous Illustrations. 8vo, Cloth, Beveled Edges, $3 00.

MACAULAY'S HISTORY OF ENGLAND. The History of England from the Accession of James II. By THOMAS BABINGTON MACAULAY. With an Original Portrait of the Author. 5 vols., 8vo, Cloth, $10 00; 12mo, Cloth, $7 50.

MOSHEIM'S ECCLESIASTICAL HISTORY, Ancient and Modern; in which the Rise, Progress, and Variation of Church Power are considered in their Connection with the State of Learning and Philosophy, and the Political History of Europe during that Period. Translated, with Notes, &c., by A. MACLAINE, D.D. A new Edition, continued to 1826, by C. COOTE, LL.D. 2 vols., 8vo, Cloth, $4 00.

THE DESERT OF THE EXODUS. Journeys on Foot in the Wilderness of the Forty Years' Wanderings; undertaken in connection with the Ordnance Survey of Sinai and the Palestine Exploration Fund. By E. H. PALMER, M.A., Lord Almoner's Professor of Arabic, and Fellow of St. John's College, Cambridge. With Maps and numerous Illustrations from Photographs and Drawings taken on the spot by the Sinai Survey Expedition and C. F. Tyrwhitt Drake. Crown 8vo, Cloth, $3 00.

OLIPHANT'S CHINA AND JAPAN. Narrative of the Earl of Elgin's Mission to China and Japan, in the Years 1857, '58, '59. By LAURENCE OLIPHANT, Private Secretary to Lord Elgin. Illustrations. 8vo, Cloth, $3 50.

OLIPHANT'S (MRS.) LIFE OF EDWARD IRVING. The Life of Edward Irving, Minister of the National Scotch Church, London. Illustrated by his Journals and Correspondence. By Mrs. OLIPHANT. Portrait. 8vo, Cloth, $3 50.

RAWLINSON'S MANUAL OF ANCIENT HISTORY. A Manual of Ancient History, from the Earliest Times to the Fall of the Western Empire. Comprising the History of Chaldæa, Assyria, Media, Babylonia, Lydia, Phœnicia, Syria, Judæa, Egypt, Carthage, Persia, Greece, Macedonia, Parthia, and Rome. By GEORGE RAWLINSON, M.A., Camden Professor of Ancient History in the University of Oxford. 12mo, Cloth, $2 50.

RECLUS'S THE EARTH. The Earth: A Descriptive History of the Phenomena and Life of the Globe. By ÉLISÉE RECLUS. Translated by the late B. B. Woodward, and Edited by Henry Woodward. With 234 Maps and Illustrations and 23 Page Maps printed in Colors. 8vo, Cloth, $5 00.

RECLUS'S OCEAN. The Ocean, Atmosphere, and Life. Being the Second Series of a Descriptive History of the Life of the Globe. By ÉLISÉE RECLUS. Profusely Illustrated with 250 Maps or Figures, and 27 Maps printed in Colors. 8vo, Cloth, $6 00.

SHAKSPEARE. The Dramatic Works of William Shakspeare, with the Corrections and Illustrations of Dr. JOHNSON, G. STEVENS, and others. Revised by ISAAC REED. Engravings. 6 vols, Royal 12mo, Cloth, $9 00. 2 vols., 8vo, Cloth, $4 00.

SMILES'S LIFE OF THE STEPHENSONS. The Life of George Stephenson, and of his Son, Robert Stephenson; comprising, also, a History of the Invention and Introduction of the Railway Locomotive. By SAMUEL SMILES, Author of "Self-Help," &c. With Steel Portraits and numerous Illustrations. 8vo, Cloth, $3 00.

SMILES'S HISTORY OF THE HUGUENOTS. The Huguenots: their Settlements, Churches, and Industries in England and Ireland. By SAMUEL SMILES. With an Appendix relating to the Huguenots in America. Crown 8vo, Cloth, $1 75.

SPEKE'S AFRICA. Journal of the Discovery of the Source of the Nile. By Captain JOHN HANNING SPEKE, Captain H.M. Indian Army, Fellow and Gold Medalist of the Royal Geographical Society, Hon. Corresponding Member and Gold Medalist of the French Geographical Society, &c. With Maps and Portraits and numerous Illustrations, chiefly from Drawings by Captain GRANT. 8vo, Cloth, uniform with Livingstone, Barth, Burton, &c., $4 00.

STRICKLAND'S (MISS) QUEENS OF SCOTLAND. Lives of the Queens of Scotland and English Princesses connected with the Regal Succession of Great Britain. Py AGNES STRICKLAND. 8 vols., 12mo, Cloth, $12 00.

THE STUDENT'S SERIES.

France. Engravings. 12mo, Cloth, $2 00.
Gibbon. Engravings. 12mo, Cloth, $2 00.
Greece. Engravings. 12mo, Cloth, $2 00.
Hume. Engravings. 12mo, Cloth, $2 00.
Rome. By Liddell. Engravings. 12mo, Cloth, $2 00.
Old Testament History. Engravings. 12mo, Cloth, $2 00.
New Testament History. Engravings, 12mo, Cloth, $2 00.
Strickland's Queens of England. Abridged. Eng's. 12mo, Cloth, $2 00.
Ancient History of the East. 12mo, Cloth, $2 00.
Hallam's Middle Ages. 12mo, Cloth, $2 00.
Hallam's Constitutional History of England. 12mo, Cloth, $2 00.
Lyell's Elements of Geology. 12mo, Cloth, $2 00.

TENNYSON'S COMPLETE POEMS. The Complete Poems of Alfred Tennyson, Poet Laureate. With numerous Illustrations by Eminent Artists, and Three Characteristic Portraits. 8vo, Paper, 75 cents; Cloth, $1 25.

THOMSON'S LAND AND THE BOOK. The Land and the Book; or, Biblical Illustrations drawn from the Manners and Customs, the Scenes and the Scenery of the Holy Land. By W. M. THOMSON, D.D., Twenty-five Years a Missionary of the A.B.C.F.M. in Syria and Palestine. With two elaborate Maps of Palestine, an accurate Plan of Jerusalem, and several hundred Engravings, representing the Scenery, Topography, and Productions of the Holy Land, and the Costumes, Manners, and Habits of the People. 2 large 12mo vols., Cloth, $5 00.

TYERMAN'S WESLEY. The Life and Times of the Rev. John Wesley, M.A., Founder of the Methodists. By the Rev. LUKE TYERMAN. Portraits. 3 vols., Crown 8vo, Cloth, $7 50.

TYERMAN'S OXFORD METHODISTS. The Oxford Methodists: Memoirs of the Rev. Messrs. Clayton, Ingham, Gambold, Hervey, and Broughton, with Biographical Notices of others. By the Rev. L. TYERMAN. With Portraits. Crown 8vo, Cloth, $2 50.

VÁMBÉRY'S CENTRAL ASIA. Travels in Central Asia. Being the Account of a Journey from Teheren across the Turkoman Desert, on the Eastern Shore of the Caspian, to Khiva, Bokhara, and Samarcand, performed in the Year 1863. By ARMINIUS VÁMBÉRY, Member of the Hungarian Academy of Pesth, by whom he was sent on this Scientific Mission. With Map and Woodcuts. 8vo, Cloth, $4 50.

WOOD'S HOMES WITHOUT HANDS. Homes Without Hands: being a Description of the Habitations of Animals, classed according to their Principle of Construction. By J. G. WOOD, M.A., F.L.S. With about 140 Illustrations. 8vo, Cloth, Beveled Edges, $4 50.

www.ingramcontent.com/pod-product-compliance
Lightning Source LLC
LaVergne TN
LVHW010219110826
845151LV00004B/1144

* 9 7 8 1 4 2 5 5 2 6 7 4 0 *